Praise for *Parts Unknown*

"Toni Niesen has landed a rapid-fire thriller with *Parts Unknown*. Set in remote and urban Alaska, her fictional adventure takes us into the inner workings of general aviation and the personalities who pursue it with passion. Protagonist, Beri Quinn, kept me turning pages late into the night."

—Elizabeth D. Nobmann, PhD, MPH, RDN, and Member, The Ninety-Nines, Inc., Alaska Chapter

***

"Great book! A suspenseful love letter to flying and Alaska!"

—Eric Bergstrom, Radio personality for Cat Country 95.1

***

"Toni Niesen has crafted a mystery as compelling as the Alaskan wilderness where it is set. *Parts Unknown* takes the reader on a twisting adventure that kept me guessing until the very end. Fans of Dana Stabenow will enjoy this new series and be asking for more. Well done!"

—Dorothy St. James, Author of the Southern Chocolate Shop Mysteries

PARTS UNKNOWN

AN ALASKAN MYSTERY

TONI NIESEN

PUBLISHING

Green Bay, WI 54311

Editor: Brittiany Koren
Copy-editor: Jessie Harrison
Cover Art Designer: Barbra Sprangers
Interior Layout Designer: Amanda Dix
Marketing: Eliza Cussen

Category: Mystery/Adventure

Description: *Can a flight instructor in the wilds of Alaska find the answers she's searching for when a plane disappears, or will she have to close shop on her flight instruction school?*

Hardcover ISBN: 978-0-9991870-2-9

Paperback ISBN: 978-0-9991870-3-6

Ebook ISBN: 978-0-9991870-4-3

LOCN: Catalog info applied for.

First Edition published by Written Dreams Publishing in July, 2017.

Green Bay, WI 54311

For my Alaska-born family, Krista, Sterling and Cole

Chapter One

July 18, 2000

The wings of the Super Cub seesawed above the terrain 1000 feet below. Buzz, my student pilot taking his second flying lesson after ground school, clutched the stick in an iron grip, his eyes glued to the runway ahead. A panoramic view of Anchorage streamed beneath us, but all I could think about was whether to let Buzz continue at the controls or to shout, "I've got it!" and take over myself.

I sat in the rear seat of my favorite taildragger, observing as the plane continued to tilt unsteadily on final approach to Merrill Field. "Buzz, you're doing fine," I said into the mic, "but you're over-correcting. Try relaxing on the controls to smooth out our landing."

"Okay, Beri," he said. "After I land the plane, I don't apply the brakes, I add power and take off again instead?"

"Correct. The tower has given you clearance for a 'touch and go'. We need to practice take-offs and landings. So what do you do next?"

He shifted in his seat. "Uh, I decrease my speed and altitude?"

Even with him speaking into his mic, I strained to hear him over the vibrations of the engine. "Yes, and remember to breathe too, please."

I watched as he descended toward the runway until the plane's tires hit concrete. We bounced twice before he went to full power, pulled the stick back and surged down the runway to take off again.

"That felt good," he said once we were in the air and he leveled off at 1500 feet. "Except for the bounces, I mean."

"You did great, Buzz. Now, let's fly to Willow and do it again."

He followed Ship Creek to the west, flew over cargo containers stacked five high at the dock of the Port of Anchorage, and started across the mud-colored waters of Cook Inlet. Denali glistened in the distance as we headed for the gardening mecca of Matanuska Valley, home of most of Alaska's prize-winning giant cabbages.

Mid-trip, the radio came alive. "This is Talkeetna Flight Service advising pilots to keep a look-out for an overdue Piper Cub. Tail number November 2789 Echo. Plane may be along your route."

I adjusted the microphone on my headset. "Please say again."

Sure enough, I'd heard the number right the first time. It was one of my planes. Fear struck me to my core.

Buzz turned in his seat and gave me a questioning glance. "Is something wrong?"

"No, you're doing a super job, but would you mind if we cut the rest of today's lesson short and started back now? I'll make up the time next lesson."

"No problem. Is that one of our planes?"

"Afraid so. I need to find out what's going on."

Buzz worked as an intern with my mechanic. He considered flying lessons a valued perk of his job.

"Our last lesson ended when the engine misfired," he said. "I'm beginning to think I'm jinxed."

"Of course you're not jinxed. That was just a magneto acting up, but we didn't want to take any chances. I'm sorry to interrupt your lessons, but I'm lucky both problems happened while I was flying with you. Most of my customers wouldn't be as understanding."

He swiveled around to glance at me. "I'll keep my eyes open for the missing plane."

We returned without spotting anything and taxied to the tie-down beside the office hangar. As Buzz cut the engine, I spotted Angie, my office manager, the folds of her ever-present tunic top rippling in the breeze against her petite frame. Why was she standing outside on the tarmac? Angie rarely emerged from inside the office except when it was time to leave for the day. Something was wrong.

The moment Buzz left the plane and entered the hangar, Angie grabbed me in a fierce bear hug. "Beri, it's Ken. He's missing."

"What? I heard flight service announce one of our Cubs was overdue. Ken's the pilot?"

"Yes. He rented the plane yesterday."

Ken Abbott was my favorite advanced student, and friend of my ten-year-old son, Jack. Ken liked to prospect for gold during his summers off from graduate school and planned to buy his own Super Cub soon. Meanwhile, he sometimes rented one of ours while he saved enough money for the purchase.

"Has anyone checked with his roommate?" I asked.

"He's out of town, but Ken's girlfriend, Shawna, says she hasn't heard from him since he left to visit one of his prospecting sites. She said Flight Service called her when he didn't close his flight plan last night."

"He probably ran into some weather and is just delayed. Where was he going?" I grabbed my flight bag from inside the plane, slammed the door and entered the office with Angie following a step behind.

"I'm not sure, but I know he planned to return yesterday evening."

"Hold on," I said once I reached my desk. "I'll call FAA to see if they've checked with local airports or heard from any pilots on his route."

I grabbed the phone from my desk and made the call, but hung up a few minutes later. "They say he filed a round-robin to Frozen Man Creek through Rainy Pass and back. The weather was poor through the pass so he probably set down somewhere to wait it out."

"I hope that's all it is," Angie said. "You might want to give Shawna a call to reassure her. She sounded scared."

Before I had a chance, Shawna pushed open the office door and walked inside.

"Beri. I'm glad you're here. I'm worried about Ken." Shawna slumped, her small frame seeming lost in the chair next to my desk. Her meticulously highlighted chestnut hair dangled in clumps from the baseball cap she'd slapped on her head. "I've been up all night. I couldn't go to sleep after I heard Ken hadn't closed his flight plan."

"Let me make you some tea, and we'll figure this out." I knew Shawna had always been nervous about Ken's flying. She'd admitted as much to me the day Ken first soloed, when we'd waited together for him to return. She tolerated Ken's flying only because she knew it was important to him.

"You know Shawna," I said, "there are lots of reasons Ken might not have closed his flight plan."

"Like what?"

"Well, start with weather. It could have changed for the worse so he decided it was too risky to fly back last night. Or, he might have encountered a mechanical problem and couldn't radio in." I handed her a steaming cup of tea. "You know he was flying a Cub?"

"He hasn't flown anything else since he got his taildragger certificate. He loves those planes." Shawna inhaled deeply of the mist rising from the Earl Grey, but set the cup down without taking a sip.

"Cubs are good machines. They've been around a long time because they're so reliable. And we both know Ken is a good pilot."

"I know that, and I know I need to relax," Shawna said, "but it's hard to do. Besides, there's something I don't understand. They said his flight plan was through Rainy Pass and back. That's not where he told me he was going when he left for the airport."

"He must have changed his mind." I clicked on my computer. "Let's check yesterday's weather report for the area."

Shawna nodded and took a sip of her tea. "I can't think of any reason he'd go that way, but if he did he would have done a last-minute weather check before he left."

I clicked to the Alaska weather report. "No, the weather was grim all day. Visibility was well below minimums at the reporting station and probably worse at the pass. I can't believe Ken would try to fly through there."

"Should that make me feel better or worse?" Shawna asked.

I fingered the chain of my locket and reached for the phone to call Flight Service. They reported there was still no word from Ken. The other two flight service stations in Alaska had nothing to offer and the plane's emergency locator beacon hadn't been activated either.

I turned to Shawna. "No luck. They confirmed Civil Air Patrol will start searching as soon as the weather in the area clears. I'll keep you posted if I hear anything."

After Shawna left, Angie pulled her chair next to mine. "Cheer up. You're right about Ken. He's probably fine. No use stewing over it yet." She gave me a thumbs-up. "Besides, I have some good news."

"I could use some about now," I said, rotating my shoulders and rubbing tension from my neck.

"Congratulations are in order. Completing that sub-contracting job with Cartos last week has put Quinn Aviation in the black," Angie said. *"Finally."*

"You're kidding." I was shocked. We hadn't been profitable in weeks. "In the black for photography or for the flight school?"

Angie gave me a smile so big that the transparent braces on her teeth gleamed. "Both. We're doing great, considering. I must admit I had my doubts you could pull it off when your dad retired, especially after you added the flight school. Hanging on to the primary business was hard enough with the economy the way it is without expanding operations."

Angie was usually the bearer of dire financial forecasts. For her, this was high praise indeed.

"We can't relax yet. We're still teetering on the edge, but our prospects are definitely brighter." She rolled her chair to her desk and returned her attention to her computer screen. "Assuming of course they find that missing plane of ours," she added.

"Thanks for the ray of sunshine. The last thing I want to do is lose the business after Dad spent most of his life building it."

I stood and walked to the door of the hangar. I needed to check on the planes before hustling over to Civil Air Patrol. We couldn't afford to waste time getting the search for Ken underway.

Chapter Two

The strong, glue-like scent of the "dope" Dean George, my chief mechanic, was using to patch the fabric of a Cessna 170, hung in the air. Dean was a forty-five-year-old Yup'ik bachelor from Bethel. He didn't talk much, but he could make an engine sing like the thrum of a baleen whale.

"Hey Dean," I said. "Problem with the 170?"

"Hangar rash," he said and nodded toward the plane. "Must have bumped it when we moved those struts yesterday."

"Shawna stopped by. She's worried because Ken didn't close his flight plan yesterday. I'm heading over to Search and Rescue to see what I can do to help. I'll probably take the twin Cessna. Those auxiliary fuel tanks we installed will extend my range. Is it in shape to go?"

"Nine-eight-tango will be ready." He looked up at me, his round face and black eyes impassive, before turning his gaze down to his feet. The glue brush in his hand already stiffening as it started to dry. "Ken, huh?"

Dean didn't show it, but I knew he was upset by the news. He and Ken were good buddies. I gave Dean a quick hug, the top of his head barely reaching my shoulder. It felt almost like hugging a muscular ten-year-old version of my son, Jack. "We'll find him, Dean."

As I left the hangar, the flat pitch prop whine from a Cessna 185 lifting off from an adjacent runway assaulted my ears, the noise nearly breaking the sound barrier. The plane belonged to a local guide service, probably ferrying a couple of tourists out for a day of wilderness fishing. Envious of their carefree plans in contrast to my dread over what our search might find, I stopped and watched the runway traffic for a moment. I stamped my foot. *No, Ken's okay. We just have to find him.* I started out in a slow jog to the opposite end of the field. Time to begin searching.

Surprise. Standing on the steps of the Civil Air Patrol building was none other than rival flight instructor, Ross McEvoy. He appeared even taller than his 6'4" frame as he stood on the top step surrounded by a group of twenty other pilots and a reporter I recognized from the *Anchorage Daily News.* Apparently, the meeting was breaking up.

"Okay folks, you've got your grid assignments," Ross announced. He brushed his curly brown hair away from his face and topped it with his cap to hold it in place. "Remember, keep in close contact. I want to know where you are at all times."

As members of the group separated and walked toward their tie-downs, I ran up the steps toward him. "Hey Ross, I came to help. Didn't realize the meeting had already started. What area do you want me to fly?"

"We've got it covered, Beri. The best thing you can do to help is to stay out of the way. Too many planes searching can cause problems. We don't need any mid-air collisions while trying to find a missing pilot."

"Be real, Ross." I was close enough to glare at him. "The search area isn't that small. We're not spotting for herring in Bristol Bay here. Just give me the coordinates, and I can fly outside your boundaries. Ken's one of my students after all."

"Maybe that was part of his problem. Like I said, we don't need your help." Ross turned and walked to the door.

I stared at his back, my hands on my hips. *Who appointed him God anyway?* We might not be close friends anymore, but his behavior was downright unreasonable. It didn't make sense not to use all available resources when a man's life could be at stake.

Chapter Three

I fumed all the way to the office. I intended to help search for Ken no matter what Ross said. Angie took one look at my scowl when I came through the door and ducked her head down to her computer screen. I sat and tried to cool down, then called the CAP office, spoke to an administrative assistant and asked her to inform Ross I planned to fly a grid on the other side of the Alaska Range, outside of any congestion in the actual pass.

Feeling better, I checked the weather, grabbed my survival vest, and confirmed with Dean that the plane was ready. I completed my checklist, filed my flight plan, and climbed aboard.

After take-off, I had time to think. Ken was easily the most outstanding student I'd ever had. He was so good, I'd planned to suggest he get his flight instructor's rating once he completed his training and built some flight hours. Jack loved Ken and did his best to wangle an invitation to tag along on a fishing or prospecting trip every time he saw him. Ken was generous with offers to take him along. He seemed to sense Jack needed a buddy to help fill the void in his life after his father and I divorced.

I spotted several search planes as I flew through the pass, and was relieved when I didn't see any evidence of a crash. Once I cleared the Alaska Range, I flew the grid I'd registered with CAP, flying at an altitude of 2500 feet. I followed streams branching from the winding Kuskokwim River, and scrutinized the flats below covered with brush and black spruce. No sign of Ken or the Cub anywhere.

Several hours and many gallons of fuel later, I reluctantly turned back and started home. Enough for one day. I'd try again in the morning after I called CAP to inform them I planned to scour the area on the other side of the pass.

Jack and I share a cedar split-entry house with my dad, Frank. It's a perfect set-up for a single mom since Dad's around to help with childcare, and he loves to cook. He's a vigorous fifty-nine-year-old, or so he says. He's said this for a number of years now, but his recollections go farther back. He stands six feet tall and carefully shaves what little hair still grows on his head. He moved in with Jack and me after my divorce. He has two passions in retirement—sports and food. Fortunately, he balances the two well and manages to stay fit despite his generous caloric intake. Unfortunately, however, he and Jack often butt heads about sports. I entered the house in time to hear Dad's baritone belting out the last stanza of the Notre Dame fight song, a rendition he usually reserved for the shower. He stood at the kitchen counter chopping onions while singing in full voice.

"Was Notre Dame a good school, Grandpa?" Jack asked.

"The best, big guy. Some of my happiest years were spent there. I was captain of the football team for two years."

"Is that where you learned how to be a pilot?"

"No, I didn't learn that at Notre Dame. That came later."

"What did you learn there?" Jack's earnest blue eyes watched Dad's every move. His oval face almost a carbon copy of my own. Maybe it was selfish of me, but it pleased me that he didn't resemble his father.

Gramps stopped chopping and dumped the onions in a sauté pan. "Oh, I mostly learned about money. How to earn money and how to manage it after I earned it."

Jack appeared to think about that for a moment, and tilted his head to one side. "Did you make lots of money?"

Dad laughed. "Enough, I guess."

"How did you make it?"

"I started a business. I flew airplanes and took pictures to make maps. The same business your mom now runs."

"Tries to run anyway," I said. "I don't seem to make as much money at it as you did."

"Don't be too hard on yourself, cupcake. My timing was good. The Alyeska Pipeline from the North Slope was under construction. A lot of development was going on and most of it required mapping. The economy is slower now."

"Is that why you retired, Gramps?"

Dad shook his head. "No, Jack. I just got too old to keep up the pace. I got tired of having to wake up early every morning to check weather over projects with no time to go fishing unless it was raining. Money isn't everything, you know. Besides, I knew your mom could step in and do a better job." He poured a bowl of shrimp into the pan, stirring quickly. "Now go wash up. I'll have dinner on the table in about five minutes."

When Jack was out of earshot, I gave Dad the news about Ken. He'd become all too familiar with missing pilots during his aviation career, and his calm words comforted me. Still, I couldn't help worrying about Ken stranded, unable to communicate and possibly hurt.

Five days later, Jack stood next to me outside the CAP building. Only his eyes moved as he watched two ravens squabbling over an open package of cheese doodles discarded from someone's lunch. A fine August rain misted the air and added an iridescent shimmer to the bird's black feathers.

Rack up one more plane crash attributed to apparent pilot error. Prevailing opinion said that Ken, anxious to get started on his prospecting weekend, flew into the pass in poor weather. It didn't make sense that he would change his original plans and fly into near-zero visibility conditions, but apparently he had. What was he thinking?

"Why Mom?" Jack asked, his eyes moist from tears. "How can they stop looking for him? They don't know for sure he's dead. Why did he have to go and crash anyway?"

I patted his shoulder. "Ken was a good pilot, sweetheart. Sometimes we don't know the answers to why things happen."

It may have been a mistake to bring Jack to the CAP press conference announcing the suspension of the search for Ken. Not that Jack gave me much choice. He'd been up and ready to leave this morning before I even showered.

"Come on, mister." I grabbed for his hand. "Let's go to the house and get some lunch."

We left Merrill Field, drove south on Gambell past the Sullivan Sports Arena and turned on Rabbit Creek Road for home. Considering Jack's mood today, it was fortunate that his grandfather wasn't home. More comfortable after changing out of our damp clothes, we nuked some leftovers for lunch and fed the scraps to Tiger, Jack's golden Labrador Retriever.

After eating, Jack slouched against the arm of the sofa. "Mom, Ken knows how to live off the land. He's real smart about that."

I smiled. "I know. Remember, a lot of us are still trying to find him. All the pilots I know are keeping a sharp eye out for his plane every time we fly near Rainy Pass. I've been re-flying some of CAP's grids every chance I get."

Jack was quiet for a moment until the phone rang. After he answered it, he tapped my arm. "Mom. Mom, can I go over to Allison's house? We want to see if we can spot a Hairy Woodpecker. She said one of her neighbors saw one in his yard yesterday."

"What does Allison's mother say?" Thanks to the resiliency of youth, Jack was finally distracted by happier thoughts.

"She said she'd call you."

"I'll be at the office. I'll tell Grandpa that I said it was okay as long as you're back in time for baseball practice."

I called and verified Dad was on his way home before brushing my shoulder-length hair and pulling it back into a ponytail. I grabbed my keys and opened the door to the garage. "Jack, please don't forget to comb your hair before you leave."

I backed my Subaru out of the garage and headed up Hillside Road toward town. It was a scenic drive with birch, spruce and scattered homes lining both sides of the pavement. Many of the houses sported colorful baskets of lobelias, marigolds and petunias hanging near the entrances, giving them a festive air that didn't match my subdued mood.

I couldn't help thinking about Ken as I drove. While it was true that I still scanned the terrain for his plane every time I flew, the odds of finding him alive were diminishing. Fast. Already the days grew shorter and the temperatures cooler. Snow would fall on the mountains in a few weeks and would be on the ground to stay in the lower elevations by Halloween.

I parked in front of the office and sat for a few moments soaking in the view of the mountains to the east. Wispy stratus clouds hung low, suspended against the purple blot of the Chugach Mountains, giving the day a cozy feel as if the sky was coming down to meet me. I parked my car and was opening the office door when a blue Audi pulled into the lot.

A tall, middle-aged woman with smooth, chin-length hair and a good tan emerged from her car and retrieved an expensive handbag from the passenger seat. She appeared more put together than my usual clientele who tended to dress in Alaskan casual.

"Quinn Aviation, right?" she asked with a distinct Boston accent.

"Sure is," I replied, and held the door open for her to enter. "What can I do for you?"

"I'm trying to locate the Quinn Flight School. Is this the place?"

"Yes, you've found us. Guess I need to update that sign." I held out my hand. "Beri Quinn."

"Beri?"

I laughed and held the door for her to walk inside. "Beryl Markham Quinn to be precise. My father had a thing for female aviators. Since my mother wouldn't consider naming me Amelia Earhart, I go by Beri." I pulled out a chair for her. "Here, won't you take a seat? I was just about to make some coffee."

The woman's eyes surveyed the length of the office with its Spartan furnishings and peered through an open door to the weather charts hanging in the classroom beyond. Her gaze finally settled on a framed photograph on my desk of several students taken at last year's Christmas party. She took a deep breath. "No coffee, thanks." She remained standing, a frown on her face. "You must have been my son's flight instructor. I'm Paige Abbott."

I sucked in my breath. *Dear God, what do I say to this woman?* Her accent should have tipped me off to her identity. Ken hailed from Boston and his speech reflected it.

"I talked to the Civil Air Patrol when Ken first went missing, and they kept me informed about the search. Now they've given up, but I still need answers. They say he made bad decisions. That wasn't like my son. Didn't you teach him proper safety protocols?"

I met her eyes. "Of course, I did. And you're right, Ken was a good student and a good pilot. He often said he couldn't understand pilots who ignored bad weather, chanced flying into '*cumulus granite*' and bragged afterward like they'd passed a test of their manhood."

"So maybe it was your plane that wasn't safe."

"No, I make sure our planes are well maintained. We have one of the best mechanics in the state who takes good care of them."

She stood her ground, unwavering. "I'm not convinced. I don't believe my son could have been as stupid as they say. If the problem wasn't your plane or your instruction, then what?"

"I don't know." I shrugged. "I'm mystified."

"You were his teacher. What are you going to do about it?"

"Do? I've been helping with the search and will continue to look for him every chance I get. I don't know what else *I* can do."

"Huh. That's obvious. You can investigate. Who better than you? You understand the system, you have the equipment and you have a stake in finding the truth." Her voice quavered. "It's damn clear no one else is going to do a thing."

She moved to the door, opened it and turned to face me. "Think about it. I'll be here to talk to you again tomorrow."

Paige Abbott was waiting for me when I arrived at the office at seven the next morning. I held the door for her and followed her into the office. Fortunately, Richard, our part-time pilot already had coffee made, so I poured us each a cup and carried them into the classroom. I motioned for Paige to follow. "Let's talk in here where there'll be fewer distractions."

"I've been thinking," she said. "I know Ken had confidence in you. I also know you have a business to run. I've decided the best way to handle this is to hire you."

"Hire me to search? I do that every time I'm in the air, but it hasn't done any good."

"I know you've tried, but I want a more extensive investigation. I understand you do aerial photography for mapping. That's something I know a little about. I'm a geologist and have experience working with aerial photos. Have you tried taking pictures of the area?"

I shrugged. "No, I haven't."

She frowned. "Well, why not?"

"The project is not well-defined. It would be very expensive to take pictures of the entire search area."

"Beri, I need you to take those pictures," Paige said, her voice firm. "Photograph every square inch of that pass. There has to be some trace of wreckage. I'll cover the expenses and pay you for your time, but get as many pictures as you can before winter comes."

I glanced at the wall calendar. "That doesn't give us long."

Her lips flattened. "I know. Time is wasting. While it may not bring Ken back, at least it will help me understand what happened. I know it would mean a lot to him not to have his reputation as a pilot destroyed, even posthumously. It would mean a lot to me as well."

"Believe me, I feel the same way, but I should tell you that the chance of reversing a verdict of pilot error is remote. Judging flying conditions is one of the pilot's most important responsibilities."

"I understand, but I'm a scientist, and scientists need explanations for anomalies. The only way I'll be satisfied is to gather all the available facts and try to make sense of them. If I know all there is to know, I think I can better accept the finality of it all."

"I hope so. I'm not sure I'll ever come to grips with losing him, but I'm praying it doesn't come to that." I finished my coffee and set my cup down.

Paige stared at me for a moment. "You said you were named after Beryl Markham. I remember now. Wasn't she the one from Africa, the one who wrote *West with the Night?* If memory serves me correctly, she found her friend when his plane was lost in the jungle. Maybe your name is a good omen for this mission."

"And I thought you said you were a scientist." I smiled. "Oh well, I guess we can use all the good omens we can get."

Paige picked up a business card from a stack on the table. "*Taildragger Flight School.* A Super Cub is a taildragger, then?"

"Yes. Ken wanted to land on sandbars so he could get into remote places without landing strips. The FAA requires a separate certification to fly taildraggers, although in my opinion it would be ideal if all pilots started their instruction with them. They'd learn better stick and rudder control that also applies to flying other types of aircraft."

19

Paige stood and wandered over to the wall by the window. She reached for a signed scrap of shirttail tacked to the sheetrock. It was surrounded by dozens of other autographed fragments, the trophies of pilots completing first solo flights. "This one was Ken's," she said, her voice husky.

"Yes, it was a proud day for both of us." I walked over to her and put my hand on her shoulder. "It's okay to cry," I said, trying to hold back my own tears.

"It catches up with me at unexpected times. Deep down, I think I'm still hoping he's out there somewhere waiting to be rescued, but I know it's wishful thinking." She clasped my hand in a hard grip and took a deep breath. "Okay, I'll pay expenses, you do the job. Do we have a deal?"

"Yes, I'll take the photos for cost, but I need to warn you that expenses will add up fast. I'll call with an estimate after I calculate the flight lines."

"Like I said, the cost doesn't matter." She picked up her purse, shook my hand one more time, and went out the door.

After Paige left, I sat at my desk feeling emotionally drained. The odds of finding Ken dead or alive weren't very high, but it would feel good to take action. I could photograph and scan the area again. It was a way to help deal with the overwhelming sense of responsibility that threatened to suffocate me. Maybe Paige could find her answers, and I could find some peace.

Chapter Four

Ten "newbie" ground school students sat around the tables in the classroom. I stood at the front of the class and brought the group to order.

"A key lesson every pilot must learn is that weather reigns supreme. It doesn't matter how important it is that you get from point A to point B before tomorrow, what matters is that you and your passengers are *alive* tomorrow."

Two of the students in the rear of the classroom glanced at each other. One yawned.

I turned to them. "Why do you think so many doctors and rock stars are killed in plane crashes?"

The kid who'd yawned flipped his hair behind his ears and shrugged. "They're rich enough to buy the best airplanes, but too busy to get proficient in them."

"Good answer. That can play a role, but the biggest reason, I feel, is that they are too schedule driven. The doctor has to return to his patients and the musician has the next gig to perform with tickets sold in advance. We'll end today's class on that thought. If you take nothing else away from our lessons, remember this: if the weather is marginal, sit it out. Stay on the ground. The risks are too great."

Angie stopped me when I emerged from the classroom. "Dean wants to see you about some kind of problem he's having."

"Thanks, I'll go see him now." I walked across the front office and through the door to the hangar. I saw Dean leaning over a Super Cub with the cowl removed, a wrench in his hand. Buzz stood beside him watching closely and holding out tools like a surgical assistant.

"Hey, Dean. Did you figure out why the engine was stuttering?" I asked.

"Yeah. It needs the left mag replaced like you thought. I used a rebuilt when I did the annual inspection because Hanratty didn't have a new mag in stock. I need to see if he has one now."

"Let me. I need to talk to him about our line of credit anyway. Angie tells me he's been insisting she pay sooner than net thirty."

"Better you than me," Buzz interjected. "That guy gives me the creeps. I don't understand why anyone does business with him."

"My dad and Ace Hanratty go back a long way. I think he's a distant cousin or something. Anyway, Dad's been a loyal customer through the years."

"I know," Dean said. "Me, I'd order online and skip the grief."

I went to the door. "We'll see how it goes. I'll let you know."

Dean spoke up. "While you're there, ask him if that cylinder assembly I ordered is in. I've been waiting almost a month." He reached over and closed the plane's cowling.

I heard the conversation continue as I left the hangar.

"Hope you'll let me watch you install that when it comes in," Buzz said.

Dean smiled. "I might even let you help."

I drove the two blocks to Hanratty's, parked, and entered the nondescript rectangle of a building. Stacks of merchandise displayed on rows of shelves lent all the charm of a big-box establishment. A buzzer sounded in the rear, and Ace Hanratty hustled up to the counter.

"Well, if it isn't Miss Quinn. In person, no less." Ace held up his right hand and rubbed his fingers against his thumb. "Got that check ready for me?"

He might be Dad's relative, but he hadn't aged as well. The flesh surrounding his eye sockets were so edematous that his eyes appeared sunken inside them. He'd soon need an eyelid lift just to see.

"Give me a break. We haven't even received your invoice. Besides, Dean's still waiting on the part he ordered. Is it in yet?" I gave him my best smile. "I need to get my plane back up in the air."

"You'll get it as soon as I do," he said. "Is that why you're here?"

"No. I want to pick up a left mag for one of the Cubs. Dean needs to replace the rebuilt one he installed. Do you have a new one in stock or should I order it on the internet?"

"Think I have one. Just a minute, I'll see." He disappeared into the labyrinth of shelving that made up the bulk of the building.

When he returned, he slid a brand-name magneto in a sealed box across the counter. "Don't expect me to supply more merchandise until we're even, hear?"

"Thanks." I signed the invoice. "Don't worry. You'll get your money. You always do."

Buzz was right. Hanratty was creepy. Maybe it was time to check out his competition. Dad may have bought his parts here for years, but loyalty should work both ways.

I climbed into the Subaru, placed the mag on the passenger's seat and was reaching to close the door when I felt a hand rest on my wrist.

"Caught you. Didn't think you saw me walking up. You were lost in thought."

"You startled me, Ross." I pulled my hand away. "You're not above talking to me now? What happened last week? All that power with the CAP go to your head?"

"You're right. I was out of line. Let me apologize and buy you breakfast. We need to clear the air about a few things."

"I ate breakfast hours ago, but coffee and a piece of pie sounds good. I'll meet you at Peggy's Café in five minutes."

The restaurant was less than a mile down the road. Painted the color of lavender eye shadow, it would be hard to miss even if it weren't located directly across Fifth Avenue from Merrill Field. After dropping the mag off with Dean, I drove to Peggy's. A favorite of pilots and most of the rest of Anchorage, the place was packed as usual.

I spotted Ross already seated in a booth near the end of the horseshoe-shaped counter. I walked past the cash register with model airplanes made from soft drink cans dangling above it and surveyed the pie case on the counter before joining him.

"See anything you liked?" Ross asked as I slid in across from him.

"Rhubarb, what else?"

"Are we ready to order or do you need a menu?" a waitress asked, notepad in hand.

"Omelet with reindeer sausage and cheddar," Ross said. "And a piece of rhubarb pie, no ice cream for the lady. Black coffee for both of us."

"Good memory," I said after she left. "Now tell me what's on your mind."

"After we eat. First, I wanted to tell you I'm sorry about Ken Abbott."

"Thanks. He's both a good student and a good friend."

"When will they learn? These young bucks don't give the weather the respect it deserves. We instructors need to emphasize that."

"You think I don't? I spend more time on weather than anything else."

"Not enough, apparently."

I slid out of the booth. "You can have my pie. I've heard enough. I should have known better than to expect you to make nice."

"Beri, stop." He reached out to block me, but I slid past and speed-walked out, dodging servers in my way.

It wasn't until I returned to the office that I realized Ross hadn't told me what he wanted to talk about.

Chapter Five

By mid-morning, the sky was blue with a hint of fall crispness in the air. I hadn't expected to have picture-taking weather today, but this was too good to ignore. The sky was severe clear over several of my pending projects. Even the weather in Rainy Pass appeared promising. I faced the pleasant, but difficult dilemma of choosing which client's job to fly first.

With arms folded across her chest and her brown eyes flashing, Angie confronted me the minute I walked through the office door. "Did you order six rolls of color aerial film from Kodak?" she asked in a louder-than-necessary voice.

"Yes. Why, have they come in already?"

"Sure did, along with an invoice for more than we have in the checking account."

"Color film doesn't come cheap. I figured my job would take at least that much, and with our need to move quickly, I wanted the film on hand. I can't re-order as I go."

"I hope you have a client's fat check that you haven't deposited yet."

I grimaced. "Not yet, although I expect to be reimbursed."

"*Expect?* You better pray it comes through. Who's the client?"

"Paige Abbott. She'll be here in a few minutes, and I don't want you glowering at her like you are at me right now. Relax. I know what I'm doing. She's agreed to pay all expenses involved in photographing the area where we think Ken's plane was lost." I gathered my notes to prepare for the meeting.

"Oh. Well, it's for Ken at least, but does she know how expensive it will be? Most people couldn't afford it."

"No, she doesn't know the exact amount, but she's a geologist. She's budgeted for mapping photography in the past so I'm sure she has a good idea."

"And if she doesn't? Who's going to pay these bills?"

"We are. I have a stake in finding Ken's plane, too. Besides, we'll put the film to good use eventually, even if she doesn't pay. I'll fill you in after I meet with her."

Angie plopped down at her desk and started entering numbers in her computer, her fingers skipping over the ten-key pad on the keyboard. I didn't know what I'd do without Angie, but some days I could strangle her.

As though on cue, Paige walked in the door. I welcomed her, introduced her to Angie and ushered her into the classroom. I shut the door to circumvent any dark glances Angie might send her way.

"Let's take a seat here at the table so you can review the map with the flight lines I've laid out." I spread the map and placed a small leather-covered weight on each corner. "A good scale is about one-inch equal to one-thousand feet. That will allow for high quality enlargements if we need them. I'm estimating the search area around Rainy Pass to be about sixty-four miles by ten miles with three offshoot drainages."

"You've put in a lot of work on this," Paige said.

"It's routine stuff in the business. I can crank it out really fast." I pointed to the lines I'd drawn. "We'd fly it at eighty-five hundred feet above mean sea level."

"That high?"

"Yes. It has to be flown above the terrain. That's how I calculated it." I picked up my notepad. "Now for the cost. I figured we'd need over eleven hundred exposures or almost six rolls of color aerial film. It could run $20,000 for the complete job and that's assuming no re-dos."

"How long will it take?"

"About three days to fly it, if the weather cooperates."

Paige glanced up from the map. "Three days. How long for processing?"

"About a week for color film with a rush order."

"Would digital photography be faster and cheaper?"

"Not really. You could hire someone with digital capability, but the processing is time consuming and costs would be higher. You'd have to pay retail prices for the photography."

"Okay then, it's almost August. When can we start?"

"This morning, I hope. If the weather holds, I'd like to get off the ground as soon as possible. The sun angle is best between eleven AM and four PM."

"I want to go with you, Beri," Paige said, rising from her chair.

I hesitated. "I'd like to take you, but there's a downside."

"Really? What's that?"

"If you go, it will mean reducing fuel to meet weight limits. We won't cover quite as much territory together."

"It's going to take more than one day to fly anyway, and I want to be part of this."

"Okay, but be prepared for a long sit. We'll be taking the twin-engine plane so plan to be aloft up to five and a half hours."

Paige smiled. "I have good bladder control. I'll just cut off the coffee."

"Why don't you pick up some sandwiches for the trip while I get the plane and camera ready? I'd like to be off the ground within the half hour."

"Will do, Captain."

After Paige left, I arranged everything I needed in the small darkroom behind the classroom before flipping off the light switch. I pulled the lid off the film can and loaded the four-hundred-foot-long film spool into the camera's magazine. After I fastened the lid, I turned on the lights, placed the magazine in my Red Flyer wagon and towed it out to the plane.

Buzz stopped sweeping the hangar floor, propped the broom against the wall and walked over to join me. "Hey Boss, can I help you with that?"

"Sure thing. Will you open the cargo door for me?" I bent my knees and lifted the forty-pound loaded magazine to the opening. "Now, climb to the rear through the passenger door, push the seat forward, and I'll slide this over to you. Watch your back, it's a bitch to get it positioned in the plane."

Buzz slid the magazine inside. "Check. Now what?"

"I can take it from here. I'll climb in and make sure it's positioned in the camera hole correctly."

"Mind if I stay? I'd like to know how you do it."

"No problem. See this lever? I use it to reset the counter for the time and date, then I make sure the light setting is right for the proper film speed." I set the dials. "That's all there is to it."

"How do you find the film speed?" Buzz asked.

"It's on the label of the film can. You get to know by the type of film you're using, but it's good to always check anyway because you can lose a whole day's work if it's wrong."

"Have you thought about going digital instead of using film?"

I laughed. "Sure, but I have to finish paying off this camera first. I'm hoping digital editing software improves and digital camera prices come down before I buy one."

"It's gotta be expensive to keep up with technology these days. The whole business is changing," Buzz said.

"You said it. The way things are going, the industry will be using unmanned aircraft before long. Pilots like me will be obsolete. Hope it doesn't happen before I get Jack through college."

We climbed out of the plane and shut the door. Buzz reached out and gave the fuselage a gentle pat. "Well anyway, thanks for the demo."

"My back should thank you." I stretched to my full height. "Actually, I'm glad to see you're so interested in the business. If you'd like, I could use a good cameraman to fly with me on some of the data-heavy jobs we do."

"You bet. Thanks."

I left Buzz in the hangar and detoured to the office to retrieve my .44 Magnum handgun, .338 Winchester rifle and ammo for both weapons from the safe. While I keep basic survival gear in all the planes, I lock up my guns after each flight. I don't consider myself *Dirty Harry* material, but if I have to make an emergency landing in the wild, I want some powerful bear protection along. Back at the plane, I slid the guns into the duffel bag containing the rest of the gear to keep them out of sight.

I slipped into my survival vest in the office, and went outside. After attaching the electric tug to the nose gear, I pulled the plane from the hangar and started my preflight checklist.

Paige returned as I finished. We climbed aboard, and Paige handed me a Fifth Avenue Deli bag.

"I bought you a diet tonic, too. Wasn't sure what you liked."

"Tonic?"

Paige smiled. "Soda. I forgot I wasn't in Boston."

"That's perfect, thanks." I stowed our lunch and reached across her to lock the cabin door.

Seatbelts fastened, throttle, props and fuel mixtures set. Master switch and mags on. After reviewing the sequence, I fired up the left engine and followed with the right. The cabin quivered with the energy of the engine vibration like a bird dog anticipating a hunt. I turned the dials on the radio. "Calling Merrill Ground. This is November 3686 Foxtrot at Quinn Aviation. Taxi for take-off with information alpha. Departing Ship Creek northwest."

"Roger. Taxi runway two-five."

After running through my take-off checklist while pausing at the end of the runway and receiving clearance for take-off, I took one last glance at the instruments to confirm they were still in the green. I moved the throttle to take-off power and the cabin rattled with the surge of the engines. The plane gathered speed down the runway until it rose into the air. The gear made a muted thunking sound as it retracted. I pulled up and made a low departure over a narrow neck of Cook Inlet to avoid air traffic from Elmendorf Air Force Base. The buildings and trees below receded as I pulled the throttles and propellers back to climb power and reached altitude.

I opened our flight plan and handed a headset to Paige, signaling that it would be easier for us to talk above the noise of the engines if she used it.

She nodded, adjusted the ear pieces and asked, "Isn't that the top of Denali I see up ahead?"

"Yes, Denali and Mt. Foraker next to it. Rainy Pass is south of them."

In silence, we drank in the scenery as we flew above the north side of Mt. Susitna, or as the locals called it, Sleeping Lady. We followed the north fork of the Skwentna River, the sunlight reflecting off the many lakes below.

The plane lurched once as we entered the pass, and the wings rocked in the turbulence caused by a light head wind. Paige seemed to relax as the plane stabilized, but we flew only a few minutes more before she turned and said, "Do you smell smoke?"

My eyes automatically went to the instrument panel, but both oil pressure and cylinder-head temperature readings were normal. I inhaled again, analyzing the scent before realizing I was smelling wood smoke. This conclusion was reinforced by the faint haziness I detected in the air below.

"The wind has shifted. We're probably running into smoke from fires in western Alaska on the other side of this mountain range."

"It's not a fire burning here in the pass?" Paige asked.

"I don't think so, but for our purposes it's still enough to make us cancel our trip. I know it's disappointing, but we can't take pictures with this much smoke in the valleys."

"Are you sure?" Paige unfastened her seat belt and leaned to peer down from the window behind her. "It doesn't seem that bad to me. We've come all this way, and I can see the ground without any problem."

"It may not appear that smoky to you, but the photos would lose definition, and we need all the clarity we can get. Now refasten your seat belt and hold on. Here we go," I said as I made an immediate right turn to the lee side of the pass.

We flew close enough to the terrain to see the fall colors of the lichen covering much of the rock wall, before turning back for home.

Paige unclenched her hands from the armrests. "I wasn't expecting anything that drastic. Do you normally fly that close to the mountain?"

"There aren't many wide passes in Alaska," I answered as I readjusted the trim. "It was plenty wide enough here to make a U-turn, but I need to fly close to the mountain on the side away from the wind to avoid downdrafts."

"Makes sense. So it's a dry run then?" Paige wiped her forehead with her jacket sleeve.

"Afraid so. Not much point in wasting film if the pictures aren't going to be any good."

"This is so frustrating. How long will it take for the smoke to clear?"

"These fires can go on for a long time. I don't know if the Bureau of Land Management is even trying to put them out. It could be perfectly clear tomorrow or it might take weeks. What we can hope for though, is a wind change."

Chapter Six

Back in the office, Paige gathered her belongings. "When I cleared Ken's things out of his apartment, I found a video of a television interview he did a couple of months ago. It was part of a local mining program where they discussed a gold nugget Ken had found. If you haven't seen the interview, you might want to see what you think."

"I'd heard he found a large nugget, but didn't see the program. It sounds interesting."

Paige pulled the DVD from her handbag and handed it to me. "I didn't make a copy so please return it when you're finished."

"Sure. Do you know where the nugget is?"

"I didn't see any sign of it at his apartment," Paige said.

"Did you ask his roommate, Nico, about the nugget?"

"I talked to him right after the plane went missing, but I didn't know about the nugget then. He's been out of town since and left me a key so I could pack Ken's stuff. Fortunately, Ken had a habit of labeling most of his possessions, but even so I couldn't always tell what belonged to Ken and what didn't."

"You might want to check with Ken's friends at the Prospectors Club. I'm sure he told them about the nugget. They might have some idea of its value."

"That's a good idea. Unfortunately, I just found out I have to fly out to Ketchikan for a few days. It's bad timing, but can't be helped. I'm leaving in the morning, but will get back as soon as I can."

"If you like, I can check to see if there's a Prospectors meeting scheduled this month."

Paige pushed her chair away from the desk and stood to leave. "Would you?" she asked. "I'd hate to lose track of Ken's nugget. It was important to him."

After Paige left, I called Alaska Mining and Diving Supply and inquired about the next Prospector's Club meeting. The person who answered informed me it was scheduled for Thursday, two days from now. Just my luck. It was the same night as the Ninety-Nines meeting I'd planned to attend. Needed to attend, really, since I was scheduled to give the scholarship committee report. The Ninety-Nines, an association of women pilots, gave scholarships to worthy students every year. It's a primary mission of the club.

I picked up my phone and called Kaitlin Rimes, the current Club president and explained my dilemma.

"It won't be a problem to put you first on the agenda," Kaitlin said. "Everyone will want to get the business meeting out of the way quickly anyway since we have an international aerobatics champion as our speaker."

"Damn, I hate to miss that myself, but thanks for your help." I hung up and slid one arm into the sleeve of my jacket when Dean walked in.

"About that magneto you bought at Hanratty's? He told you it was new?"

I disentangled myself from my jacket and sat down. "Yes, I told him you were replacing the rebuilt one."

"Well, the only thing new about it is the packaging. It's another rebuilt, just "stripped and dipped" to make it appear new. It didn't have a FAA yellow tag attached."

"No kidding." I was shocked. "I'll talk to him first thing tomorrow."

"Don't bother. I already gave Ace a piece of my mind. He swore he sold it to you as a rebuilt."

"He's mistaken. Besides, it's illegal to sell rebuilt parts without the required tag. I'll file a complaint with the FAA on my way home tonight. Enough is enough." I grabbed my jacket and stood to leave.

"Let me know what you figure out. I'll need to get that part soon," Dean said and turned back toward the door to the hangar.

I glanced at my watch. Enough time to get to the FAA office if I hurried. Angie had already gone to pick up her kids from the Boys and Girls Club so I flipped the sign on the door to "Closed" and locked up early. I tried not to think what Dad would say. He was a stickler for professionalism at work. He would have been mortified.

As I drove the short distance to the FAA Building, I thought about my visit to Hanratty's. That mag was packaged to appear new. How long had he been cheating his customers? While I was thinking about it, I pulled over, got out my phone and called Northern Airparts and asked about getting another mag.

"You're in luck," the voice on the line said. "We've had trouble keeping them in stock, but we do have one left. Do you want me to hold it for you?"

"Please. Hold it under Quinn Aviation. One of us will pick it up first thing tomorrow."

The door to the FAA building was kept security-locked. I pushed the button of the intercom box beside it. "May I help you?" a voice asked.

"Yes, I hope so. I want to file a report regarding a problem I've encountered with an aircraft part."

"Do you have an appointment?"

"No. I didn't realize I'd need one to register a complaint. Can I pick up some forms?"

"We're getting ready to close, but we do have one staff person still here who could help you." The lock on the door buzzed.

I pulled the door open, and the receptionist waved me to a counter on my right. A young man came from around the corner to greet me.

"Hi there," he said, a smile on his face. "Hear you want to file a report?"

I explained the situation and asked, "Have you heard of problems like this from anyone else?"

"No, not in Alaska, but then I just transferred here from the lower forty-eight last month." He pulled some forms from a drawer. "Are you sure it was a rebuilt mag? Do you still have it?"

"We have it. I can bring it in if you like."

"Not necessary. We'll send our inspector around. He'll want to talk to your mechanic anyway." He glanced at the clock and handed me several pieces of paper. "Guess it's time to close up. Just complete these and drop them off tomorrow."

I took the forms and started home. It had been a long day, and I was anxious to spend some quiet time with Jack.

As I turned on Rabbit Creek Road, I left most of commercial Anchorage behind me. The spruce trees here were full-sized and lent a summer-camp atmosphere to the area. I felt my shoulders fully relax when I reached our unpaved street and drove by my neighbor's log house. I pushed the button on the remote to open my garage door and drove inside.

The scent of garlic and onions engulfed me as I walked into the house from the garage. "Do I smell something Italian cooking?" I took a deep breath. "Whatever it is, it smells wonderful."

I tripped over Tiger stretched out blocking the kitchen door.

"Lasagna and garlic bread. Hope your appetite's hearty. I made enough for an army," Dad said.

"I'm famished. Seems like lunch was a long time ago." As I passed through the kitchen, I gave Dad a hug and grabbed an olive from the salad he was tossing. I was lucky to have him to rely on. "Think I'll take a quick shower before dinner. My clothes smell like smoke after flying through Rainy Pass today."

"Wild fires, huh? You go ahead. Jack should be home soon and then we can eat."

Scrubbed and freshly shampooed, I pulled on a clean UAA Seawolves sweatshirt and a fresh pair of jeans before descending the stairs to the kitchen. "Still no Jack?" I asked.

Dad turned to face me after he finished pulling plates from a cabinet. "He called. Said he would be just a few more minutes."

"This might be a good time to ask you about the phone call I got yesterday from a football league. They said I owe them $100 for Jack's registration."

"Yeah, that's right. I wanted to get the paperwork in before the deadline."

"And last week the hockey club called, also wanting money."

"So?"

"So Dad, you can't just go around town signing Jack up for things I know nothing about."

He slid a foil-covered loaf of garlic bread into the oven and shut the door. "I haven't had a chance to tell you."

"The problem isn't really the money, it's that Jack isn't interested in most of these programs. He's not the sports-oriented person you are."

"He needs to stay busy, sweetheart. He needs the exercise. He spends most of his time glued to a book or computer game, and the rest of the time he's over at some girl's house watching birds. No grandson of mine is going to end up as a sissy birdwatcher!"

I sat down at the breakfast bar. "I'm glad you want the best for Jack, but if you push him too hard he'll lose interest in all sports. Besides, there's nothing sissy about bird watching. I'd challenge you to go hiking with some of the birders I know."

Tiger leaped up, tail wagging furiously and ran to the door. Jack walked in a few seconds later.

He set his backpack down on the floor. "Hi Mom, Gramps. Smells awesome in here. When do we eat?"

"Right now, son. Wash your hands, and you and your mom can dig in. I'm not going to join you for dinner tonight. Sarah is cooking beer-battered halibut. I'm supposed to be there at seven so I need to hustle and get ready."

"Hmmm, this is starting to get serious." I said, a smile playing on my lips.

"Don't be silly. She caught her limit on a charter out of Homer and says it doesn't make sense to fry up just a little. She's invited a bunch of people."

"You might consider taking her a side dish of lasagna. There's no way Jack and I can eat all this, although it was wonderful of you to make it for us."

"Not a bad idea. I'll cover this pan and take it with me. Don't wait up," Gramps said, "not that I'll be that late."

After dinner, Jack turned on his computer, and I sat down to fill out the FAA forms and review my ground-school notes for tomorrow's class. I didn't like to admit it, but Ross's comment about my teaching had struck a nerve. Maybe I could stress the importance of weather decisions even more than I had in the past.

It wasn't long before I grew restless, put the class folder away and threw a load of laundry in the washer. Returning to the den, I picked up the video Paige had given me that I'd brought in from the car. I turned on the television, popped the DVD in the machine and pushed a couple of buttons on the remote.

Ken Abbott's picture immediately filled the screen. He held a large gold nugget up for the television camera.

"How big is this nugget you found?" the interviewer asked.

"It weighs a little over five troy ounces," Ken said, and handed it to the anchor.

The man hefted it up and down in his palm. "A whopper! Does it set any records?"

"Not really, but for me, it's the find of a lifetime," Ken said, returning the chunk of gold to a leather pouch and slipping it into his pocket. "The largest nugget found in Alaska weighed almost three hundred troy ounces, but this was a real coup for an amateur like me."

"And where did you say you found it?"

"I didn't say. I don't want to start a modern-day gold rush." Ken grinned at the camera in a way that brought a catch to my throat. "I'll tell you this much. The place is fly-in only, and I found it using very low-tech mining equipment."

"What did you use, a gold pan?"

"Yes and no. Last fall I located a fast-moving stream and placed some fiber doormats in a spot I thought was promising. This summer after the snow melted, I flew out, collected my mats and panned the sediment from them in a tub in my back yard," Ken said.

"So you trapped the nugget in a welcome mat and panned it at home?"

"Well, this nugget actually landed on top of one of my mats. It was a fluke. All you can expect to pan from the mats is gold dust or flake gold, and that's if you're lucky," Ken leaned in toward the camera and grinned. "You're more likely to find nuggets with a metal detector."

"Can you go out and explore for gold in any stream in Alaska?"

"No, first you check to make sure you're not claim jumping."

"How about permits?"

"You don't usually need a permit for recreational mining, but you can check the state website or call the Sourdough Prospectors Club for details," Ken said.

"There you have it folks," the interviewer concluded. "It seems there's still some gold in them 'thar' hills. Or maybe I should say in 'them streams'. Tune in next week for more about real-life adventure in this great state of ours."

I clicked the television off and ejected the disk. When I turned, I saw Jack standing behind me wiping his eyes with his sleeve.

"I wonder why Ken didn't tell me about finding a nugget," Jack said, sounding hurt. "I even helped him prospect for gold once."

"He probably didn't get the chance," I said, giving Jack a hug and tousling his hair. "I'm sure you would have heard all about it the next time you saw him. Bet he'd want you to be one of the first people he showed it to."

"I hope you find him soon, Mom," Jack said. "I miss him, and I want him to give me all the scoop on that nugget."

"I hope so too, sweetheart."

Chapter Seven

The next morning I dressed quickly and made a beeline for the garage. I planned to start work earlier than usual today.

Wearing his usual flannel and jeans, Dad held out an arm and stopped me. "Whoa. What's going on? No breakfast?"

"No time. The weather is good in Kenai, and I want to get an early start on a small job there. If I can finish it before noon and the wind cooperates in Rainy Pass, I may be able to get some photos there today, too."

Dad handed me a muffin. "Here, you can eat this on the way."

"Thanks." I grabbed a napkin. "Can you feed Jack tonight? I may be late."

"Sure, no problem."

I parked outside the hangar and made haste to get off the ground. Luckily, the wind wasn't blowing out of Turnagain Arm this morning as it often does. The flight was smooth and uneventful. I scanned the ground for wildlife as I flew over the Kenai National Moose Reserve, but all I saw was a group of people in canoes setting off on one of the small interconnecting lakes. The area is accessible by road, unlike many areas of Alaska, making it perfect for Boy Scouts' activities and other outdoor adventure seekers.

I radioed Kenai Tower fifteen miles out from my destination. "This is 4198 Tango. I'm scheduled for aerial photography over Kenai Airport at 1400 feet. It's five flight lines and will take less than twenty minutes."

"This is Kenai Tower. Can't let you proceed at your altitude. We have conflicting traffic. Can you go higher?"

"That's negative. I have to fly it for mapping scale. How long a delay do you expect?"

"We'll be busy at least until early afternoon."

"Damn!"

The dispatcher had told me there wouldn't be a problem when I'd called this morning or I wouldn't have flown down. I could return to Anchorage or sit it out here on the ground and hope I could get my pictures before I lost the sun angle needed. I decided to take my chances and wait.

I descended over Nikiski and the oil refinery where oil is pumped onshore from platforms in Cook Inlet. Kenai sits on the north shore along the Kenai River, a favorite sports fishing destination. Below, fishermen were drift fishing for silver salmon and casting flies for dolly varden and rainbow trout. Carcasses of humpies and sockeye from earlier salmon runs littered the river banks. This time of year, the trout were so sated with spawned-out salmon and salmon eggs they paid scant attention to the flies.

Kenai Airport was small, with just one runway and an adjacent seaplane landing and parking area, but it was large enough to boast a tower, several charter services, a flight service station and a pint-sized public terminal.

After landing, ground control directed me to transient parking. I tied down and walked to the flight service searching for coffee. Sure enough, a fresh smelling pot was on, and three guys were on duty. One was talking on the radio, another was shooting the bull with a pilot, and a third was tilted back in his chair, a baseball cap covering his eyes.

"Hey Vic," I said, yanking his cap further down to his nose. "Wake up. No sleeping on duty."

"Big Red!" Vic straightened his lanky frame and pushed his cap up on his head. "To what do I owe the pleasure, stranger?"

"Will you please stop calling me Big Red? One disastrous make-over attempt after my divorce, and you won't let me live it down." I lowered myself into a chair next to his desk. "Never again. My hair will stay the same butterscotch brown until the day it turns gray. Actually, I dropped by hoping for a cup of coffee. The tower wouldn't give me clearance to take my pictures so I thought I'd visit you and hope for a break in the action."

"What action? It's been slower than waiting for soccer goals around here. Everyone's holding off for the fishing to improve. You must have encountered Hap on the mic." Vic screwed up his face in an exaggerated wink. "Nothing happens with Hap on duty. Makes him work too hard. He'll probably stall you till his shift change."

"Wonderful," I said. "When would that be?"

"Not until around three. Here, let me stir things up for you. I'll give a call to the shift supervisor, and I bet we can get him to reconsider."

"Hold up, Vic. I don't want to make an enemy. I may be back this way one of these days."

Vic shrugged. "Who's your customer? Maybe I can deflect the blame."

"Believe it or not, the contract is for the FAA. It's a design project to upgrade navigational facilities and check clearances for approaches to the airport."

"Perfect. How can he be mad at the FAA?" Vic picked up the phone, called the supervisor, and turned to me with a conspiratorial wink. "No problem," he said, hanging up the receiver.

"Call the tower in about fifteen minutes, Red. You should be all set."

I rolled my eyes at the name, but said, "I owe you one. Thanks."

Vic and I went way back. Our dads were best friends and we'd spent much of our childhood together camping and fishing with them.

"I'll collect next time I'm in Anchorage. You can buy me a beer." He stretched his arms in front of his chest, fingers interlocked. "How's business these days?"

"I'm keeping busy. A few more problems than I'd like, but I guess that's life."

"What kind of problems?"

I filled him in on Ken's missing plane and the search being called off. "It doesn't look good."

"I did hear about that, but didn't realize he was a student of yours. That's a tough one. Are you still searching on your own?"

"Yes, I've been searching as often as I can. On top of that, I've been having problems keeping my planes in the air. Parts for my Cubs are scarce. I've had trouble getting them, and some I have managed to buy have been mislabeled." I stood to leave.

"Mislabeled? Funny, someone else mentioned a problem with parts not long ago. Tell me about it while I walk you out." He stopped outside the building and scanned the area. "Where're you parked?"

"Transient parking, where else?" I waited for him to catch up before walking to the plane. "We recently bought a new mag for one of the Cubs. It was packaged and sold as new, but it turned out to be rebuilt. I reported it to the FAA, but haven't heard anything from them yet."

Vic paused and snapped his fingers. "I remember who it was now. A guy who comes through here fairly regular in his Super Cub. Has a cabin in the area, I think. Anyway, he said he thought there might be a chop shop for airplane parts operating somewhere around here. I'll keep my ears open and let you know if I hear anything more."

"I'd appreciate that, Vic." I gave the plane a quick once over, climbed in and contacted the tower. This time there were no complaints about diverting traffic for me. I'm not sure how critical the project was for the FAA, but with the bureaucracy and the weather in sync, it took only ten minutes to finish the job.

I walked into the office to find Angie standing at the counter talking to a rail-thin young man.

"Oh, here she is now. Beri, this is Owen Krenshaw. I just signed him up for your October ground school."

I reached out and shook his hand. "Welcome. Glad to meet you," I said.

"Same here. I'm anxious to get started so I can be ready for next year's hunting season." He gave me a thumb's up and pushed against the door to leave. "See you in October."

I turned to Angie. "October ground school?" I asked. "I don't remember scheduling that."

"You didn't," Angie said, "but you needed to. It's that time of year."

"I don't know about him. His expectations sounded unrealistic."

"Well, he may need to slow down a little, but you can handle that when the time comes." Angie snapped the class schedule book closed. "By the way, I rescheduled the instrument student on your calendar tomorrow to be with Richard instead. He was in earlier and was okay with the change. He wants more hours anyway, and I thought it was a good idea with you being so tied up with Ken's mother and all."

She turned and busied herself straightening a pile of papers on her desk, a deflecting strategy she used when she knew she was getting pushy.

This time, she'd had a good idea. Richard Toledo, a retired Air Force pilot worked with us part-time. He was an excellent flight instructor and relief pilot, and I did need to free up my schedule. Besides, I wasn't quite ready to jump into flight instructing. Ken weighed on my mind too much.

"One more thing," Angie said, "did you receive an expense check from Paige yet?"

"Afraid not." I stuffed my Kenai maps in the battered filing cabinet next to my desk. I carried the maps as back-up since I'd loaded them on my laptop as well. "But I did finish the Kenai job. You can bill it as soon as we receive the prints from the lab."

Angie nodded her approval as she tapped the keys of her computer to enter the completed job in her spreadsheet.

"Did you notice that message from the CEO of Cartos, the outfit that's been sending us those subcontracting jobs lately? He sounded anxious to talk to you and even asked you to call his *personal* number. And Beri, if I remember right, he's very handsome." She arched an eyebrow at me and smiled.

"Alex Veronin?" I flipped through my messages until I found the right one and dialed his number.

He picked up on the second ring. "Beri, thanks for getting back to me. Good work on that last job. Our client was pleased."

"Great. Weather conditions couldn't have been better for the project."

"I called because I have a proposition for you. I'm going to be in Anchorage two weeks from now and wondered if you would accompany me to a gala for the Kids Are Our Future group? It's a mandatory attendance function for me, and I thought we could discuss some business decisions we have coming up and score some PR points, too."

"I'm not big on society functions, but if it's good for business I'll do my best."

He chuckled. "Knew I could count on you. I'll send you the particulars when I get them."

I disconnected and sat wondering if it was business he had in mind. Angie was right. No question he was an attractive man. I'd only met him in person once before, but his magnetism was undeniable. The way he gazed into my eyes without blinking made me squirm. I felt much more comfortable conducting business with him at a distance. Still, an evening with Alex *could* prove interesting.

Chapter Eight

The Ninety-Nines' meetings were held in one of the University of Alaska Aviation Department's classrooms on the east end of Merrill Field. Since it was just down the street from my office, I arrived a few minutes early. I entered the lobby and crossed under the three small airplanes dangling from the vaulted ceiling toward the meeting room. I smelled the coffee brewing before I opened the door and saw Cheryl Johnson, a UA instructor and long-time Ninety-Nines member, seated alone at a table.

"Hi Cheryl. Where is everybody? I expected to see a crowd tonight."

She smiled, her crooked grin transforming her otherwise unremarkable features. "You're just early. Kaitlin asked me to fill in for her. She mentioned you wanted to be first on the agenda tonight."

"Yes, unfortunately I need to make a quick getaway. What's up with Kaitlin?"

"She planned on being here right up to a couple of hours ago when she got word her new plane had been stolen. She's talking to the police."

"*Stolen?* Where did this happen?"

"Right off the Birchwood Airstrip. She tied it down there for a couple of days while she had ski mounts installed. It's so sad. She'd waited months for the plane to be delivered and barely got to fly it before it was taken."

"A tough break," I said. "What kind of plane was it?"

"I'm not sure what Kaitlin ended up buying. She was deliberating between a Maule and a Cub last I heard."

"Let's find out the particulars so we can all keep a look-out for it." I grabbed a donut and washed a bite down with coffee.

"Nice idea, but it's probably in Canada or some third world country by now." Cheryl handed me a promotional catalog and pointed to a picture of a form-fitting Ninety-Nines t-shirt. "We should place an order for our fundraiser in January. Kaitlin said she'd dealt with them in the past, and they have good stuff. She has samples of decals with our logo. There's one on the last page."

I flipped through the catalog while people straggled into the room. I wasn't as impressed as Cheryl. It featured the kind of junk that cluttered my cabinets at home. The designs were attractive, but how many coffee mugs, lanyards and decals can a person use?

Cheryl finally called the meeting to order, and I reported the committee's recommended recipients for our annual scholarship awards. We choose a promising aviation student to receive a full tuition scholarship to UAA and waive fees for two students to attend the winter survival class I help teach. We were late making the awards this year, so I was pleased our selections were approved. It would be a relief to get the award letters in the mail.

The guest speaker arrived just as I finished. I said a quick hello to her and excused myself from the meeting.

Fortunately, the Prospectors Club held meetings at Alaska Mining and Diving Supply located only a few blocks away. I'd never been inside the building before so threaded my way through displays of metal detectors and snow machines in search of the meeting room. A muscular young man caught my eye and called, "You trying to find the prospectors? The meeting's through there." He motioned to a corridor I hadn't noticed.

I followed the rumble of voices to a conference room and stood for a moment inside the doorway, observing about thirty people clustered in small groups. Their conversations bounced against my ears, a jumble of words, loud, but unintelligible. I scanned the room to see if I knew anyone. Unfortunately, I did.

"Beri!" Gracie Higgins brayed in her too-loud voice. Her red, frizzy hair bounced as she met me halfway. She's my age, but shorter. "What the devil are you doing here? I can't imagine you digging through gravel, you might chip a nail." She leaned forward laughing at her own attempt at a joke.

If it were anyone else, I'd be convinced she'd been drinking, but Gracie had been obnoxious since I first met her in grade school. She's pushy with no social skills whatsoever.

"Hi, Gracie. No, I haven't taken up digging for gold. I came to see if I could meet some of Ken Abbott's prospecting friends."

"Ken? Everybody knew him. What do you think caused him to crash anyway?"

"I don't know for sure what happened to him. I wish I did. Who do you think he was closest to in this group?"

"Well," she scanned the faces in the room, "you might try Wally over there. I know he and Ken sat together at meetings sometimes."

"Thanks, Gracie." I moved swiftly across the room hoping she wouldn't follow.

"Hey, wait up," she said, following in my wake. "I'll introduce you."

"That's okay. I think I know him," I said and moved faster.

"Wally? I'm Beri Quinn. Haven't I seen you around Merrill Field?"

He turned and smiled, the corners of his eyes crinkling. "Yeah, I have my Cessna parked there." He was about my height and stocky with an open, friendly face.

"Glad to meet you. I came tonight to talk to some of Ken Abbott's friends and Gracie tells me you knew him well."

"Yeah, Ken was a great guy," Wally said. "Hey, the meeting's getting started. Maybe we can talk afterward."

"Thanks," I said. "I'd appreciate that."

State and federal permitting laws for hand-held dredging devices, the topic on the agenda tonight, generated a lot of heated discussion. What I got out of it was that the club members didn't like too many government rules.

When the meeting ended, Wally steered me to a corner quiet enough for conversation. "What was it you wanted to know about Ken?"

I explained that Ken's mom was curious about the whereabouts of the nugget he'd found.

"That was quite a nugget," he said. "It had great color and a distinctive shape. Everything you could want in a nugget. I don't know where it is, but it would be easy to recognize. It's shaped like the state of Indiana."

"Did Ken mention his plans for the nugget?"

"Afraid not. I knew he agreed to be interviewed on television, but I didn't see the show. I don't even know where he found it."

"I don't think anyone does. Do you know about what it was worth?"

"More than just its weight. Natural nuggets are mostly used by jewelers to make custom pieces. Guess you could check with one of the local shops downtown."

"Can you think of anyone here who might know more about it?"

"Not really." He thought for a moment. "Well, maybe Norm Underwood. He's not here tonight, but I can give you his cell number."

"Thanks," I said, as we walked out to the parking lot. "You have a lively group here."

"Yeah, you don't fall asleep in these meetings." He laughed and walked across the parking lot.

"Gracie followed close behind me. I hopped in my car and turned the key in the ignition.

"Beri!" Gracie called. "Wait up. I hoped we could stop for coffee and catch up."

"I'm sorry, Gracie. That would be nice, but I need to get home. I haven't seen my son all day. Maybe some other time." I put the car in reverse.

"Wait!" Gracie cried, waving her arms in the air. "Wait. You have a flat tire."

I turned off the ignition and got out to inspect it. Sure enough, the rim of the rear tire on the driver's side rested on the pavement.

"I hope my spare's in good shape," I said, lifting the rear hatch and pulling out the spare.

Gracie grabbed it and bounced the tire a few times to check the air pressure. "Looks like it's okay."

I'd just pulled out my jack when Gracie spoke.

"Uh oh," she said.

I stared in her direction. "What do you mean, uh oh?"

"Your other tire is flat, too," she said.

"You just tested it. It's okay." I gave it another bounce for emphasis.

"I mean your other rear tire," she replied. "I didn't notice before because another car was parked next to you on that side."

"You're kidding." I dropped the tire iron in disgust, examined both tires and reached into the car to get my cell phone from my purse. As I leaned inside, something white under the passenger side windshield wiper caught my eye. I got out and pulled the scrap of paper from beneath the blade. On it, someone had written in bold letters, ***Back off!***

"What does it say?" Gracie asked, leaning over my shoulder to read it. "What does it mean?"

"I have no idea, but I don't like it. I'm calling the police."

Chapter Nine

I woke the next morning feeling as if I hadn't been to bed. The police had been slow to respond and weren't optimistic about finding the vandal who had targeted my car. The tow truck I called after they left wasn't any speedier. Thankfully, Gracie had stayed and given me a ride home. She'd been a big help last night. I felt a little ashamed of myself for misjudging her in the past.

I picked up the business card she'd given me before she left and glanced at it before slipping it in my address book. *G.L. Higgins, Attorney-at-law, Specializing in Family Law.* That was a surprise. I'm not sure what profession I'd expected, but it seemed a good fit. She'd always loved to talk.

Dad dropped me off at the mechanic's shop to pick up my car. As soon as I parked it at the hangar, I hurried in to get the airplane ready. The weather service predicted good weather and light wind in the Rainy Pass area. I was anxious to get started.

The trip went well, and I finally got some pictures. I returned to the office feeling I'd made a sizable dent in the flight lines I'd laid out. Paige would be happy.

I called the FAA office to confirm that the report I'd dropped off had been received by the appropriate person. The receptionist assured me it was already making its way through the official channels. I clicked off and the phone instantly rang. Ross's number popped up on the caller ID. Good. I wanted to talk to him.

"Hi. Thought I saw you land a few minutes ago," Ross said. "Seems like I always need to apologize to you, and I *am* sorry. I didn't mean to insult you the other day at Peggy's."

"Apology accepted. I over-reacted, and I'm sorry, too." The eraser of the pencil I held bounced against the surface of my desk and I willed myself to stop the nervous mannerism. "I never did find out what you wanted to talk to me about."

"It's complicated. How about we go to the salmon bake at Chester's hangar tomorrow afternoon? It will help to be well fed for the conversation I have in mind."

"Sounds good. I should be able to make it unless I'm flying. I'll call you if that's the case. Any hints in the meantime?"

"Sorry again. I'll fill you in tomorrow."

I disconnected and readied my exposed film for shipping. I hoped this batch of pictures would yield clues to Ken's whereabouts. I jotted the salmon bake on my schedule and left to pick up Jack at the ball park.

I worried that Jack needed a dad. His granddad helped, but since the divorce, Jack rarely saw Dennis. Even before he moved out and left us, Dennis was out of town most of the time. He'd never spent much time with his son.

I met Dennis in high school while I was dating Ross. Whether I was flattered by the competition for my attention or it was true love, I'll never know, but I fell hard at the time. Dennis thought it was a hoot to date a girl who flew airplanes, but as soon as I said "I do" he was dead set against my working as a pilot. We fought this battle for ten years until my thirtieth birthday when he left to be with his girlfriend in Arizona. Now they're married.

I turned off the Old Seward Highway on O'Malley Road, driving past the Anchorage Zoo. As I made the turn, I scanned the cars behind me to make sure I wasn't being followed. I had no idea how the person who vandalized my car last night knew where to find me, but I had to assume it was either someone from the meeting or someone who had followed me there.

I didn't see anyone suspicious so I pulled into the parking lot of the Abbott O'Rabbit Baseball Field. Stunted black spruce trees grew in the marshy land behind the field ringed by fuchsia-colored fireweed growing along the edge of the fence and the roadway.

Jack stood apart from a small group of players. He was shorter than most of his team, probably due for a growth spurt soon. He spotted my car and trotted over. "You're late, Mom."

"Not really," I said. "Your practice must have ended early."

"Maybe we need to synchronize watches," Jack said under his breath.

"I heard that. We'll check them when we get home. Is everything else okay with you?"

"I'm fine." His fingers picked on the lacing around the edge of his fielder's mitt.

"You know, you're going to totally unlace your glove if you keep messing with it. Seems to me, something's bothering you."

"Not really. I'm just thinkin'."

"Tell me what you're thinking about then."

Jack glanced my way then down at his glove. "Mom, can't you give it a rest? Please?"

"No Jack, I can't. We moms worry, you know."

Jack made a fist and punched his glove. "Okay, I was just wondering if maybe I was adopted or something."

"Adopted?" Wow, that was the last thing I expected. "Whatever gave you that idea?"

"You know Eva in my class? She's adopted and she doesn't look anything like her parents."

"That's because she's Chinese, and they're not. Her parents adopted her from an orphanage in China, but what's that got to do with you?"

"Well, I don't look much like you or Dad."

"You don't? I always thought you inherited my best features." I gave his shoulder a quick shove, hoping to get a smile from him.

Jack turned to me with a serious expression on his face. "Can't you see? I have blonde hair, and both you and Dad have brown."

"Oh," I said. "Well if it makes you feel any better, my hair was blonde when I was your age, and I can personally attest to the fact that you're not adopted. The day you were born was the happiest day of my life."

"Okay. That's good, I guess." Jack's eyes focused back on the mitt in his lap.

"You guess? Jack, what's really going on here? Are you worried about something else?"

"I just thought if I was adopted, that might be why Dad doesn't like me."

"Sweetheart, your dad likes you. He loves you very much."

"Well, he doesn't ever come to see me."

"I know. It's hard with him in Arizona. Tell you what, let's give him a call tonight. It would be good for you two to talk more often."

"Can I? Do you think he'll want to talk to me?"

"Of course he will, if he's home. I can't promise that he will be, but it's worth a try. He'll be happy to hear about what you've been up to." I pulled the Subaru into the garage and cut the engine. "You hop out and make sure Tiger has food and water."

"Okay." Jack bounded out of the car, slammed the door and ran inside.

I sat a little longer, thinking about how to approach Dennis. Our relationship was civil, but just barely, and his current wife hadn't tried to disguise her dislike for me the few times we'd talked. God only knows what stories Dennis had told her. I ached for Jack. My memory of my own feelings of rejection after my mother deserted our family would always be with me.

The house was quiet when I stepped inside, and I didn't smell anything cooking. Apparently, Dad wasn't home yet. Good. Calling Dennis would be dicier with him badmouthing Dennis in the background.

I poured a glass of Chardonnay before picking up the phone. The glass felt cold on my fingers, and I rested it a moment against my forehead before pushing the buttons on the phone.

"Hello, Dennis. Yes, all is well with us. I called because I have a young man here who wants to talk to you."

I held out my hand. "Jack, your dad is on the phone." He ran to grab the receiver. After he answered, I walked into the kitchen, started rearranging cans in the pantry and pretended I wasn't eavesdropping.

"Dad, I know. I miss you, too. I miss you a lot."

Dennis must have been doing most of the talking since there wasn't much to hear on this end. After about five minutes, Jack piped in. "Yeah, that would be great! Could I?" He turned his body facing away from me and lowered his voice. "Okay, I'll talk to her. When should I let you know? Okay. Love you. Bye." Jack clicked the phone off and set the receiver down. He seemed lost in thought for a moment, then turned and rushed to me in excitement.

"Guess what, Mom? Dad wants me to come visit him. Can I? Can I, huh?"

"School doesn't start for a few more weeks so I don't see why not. Did he mention any dates?"

"No, he said he'd check with the airlines and call me. I *really* want to go, Mom."

I ruffled his hair. "I kinda figured that. We'll see what we can work out."

"What's up?" Gramps asked as he walked in from the garage carrying a bag of groceries.

"I'm going to go visit Dad," Jack exclaimed. "I just talked to him on the phone."

"August in Arizona. That should be wonderful," Gramps said. "Hey, I picked up cold-cuts for dinner. Didn't have time to cook tonight. How does chicken breast, Provolone and pesto on a baguette sound? I bought a melon for dessert."

"Yum," I said, washing my hands. "Let me put things together while you take a load off your feet and catch the news on television." I took the bag and started unloading the contents. "Mmm, Greek olives, too."

"You've got a deal," Dad said as he walked through the door to the den.

"Don't make mine, Mom. I'd rather make my own sandwich."

"You're on. I'll just put everything out on the table."

"What did Gramps mean about August in Arizona?" Jack asked. "He didn't sound very happy for me."

Although I wasn't thrilled with the idea of Jack taking the trip, I put on a happy face for him. "Oh, it's just that it's hot in the desert this time of year, that's all. We'll have to buy you a couple of pairs of shorts and some sandals for the trip. If only I could resolve my own doubts.

Chapter Ten

Norm Underwood, Ken's friend from the Prospectors Club, agreed to meet me at nine PM on the Second Street Trailhead to the Tony Knowles Coastal Trail. Turns out he worked for the FBI and made it a priority to stay in shape with daily exercise, a plan I would be wise to adopt. I love the extended daylight hours of Alaska's summers—more time to play, even if it meant less time to sleep. Tonight we had perfect running weather with the temperature in the mid-sixties and just enough breeze to keep the mosquitos away.

Norm stood off to the side of the trail stretching his legs. He was easy to identify by the yellow fanny pack he'd said he would wear. With a thick-muscled body and a slight pudge around his middle, he didn't have the appearance of a habitual runner.

"Hi," I said and held out my hand to shake. "Beri Quinn. You must be Norm."

"That's me. Glad to meet you." He gripped my hand with enthusiasm and appeared anxious to get started.

"Do you run often?" he asked, eyeing my jeans and tee. At least my Asics running shoes would pass muster.

"Not as often as I should. I prefer hiking or racquetball, but I'll try to keep pace with you until the first rest area where I'll turn back."

"You said this was about Ken Abbott. What is it you want to know?"

"Ken's plane has been missing several weeks now, and the search for him was called off." I started a few stretches of my own while I talked. "Meanwhile, I've been working with his mother to continue searching."

"You said you were looking for the nugget he found. What's your angle on that? Is the nugget missing, too?"

"Yes, Ken's mom's been clearing his things out of his apartment and hasn't seen it. She's curious about it and thought his friends from the club might know something."

We started at a slow pace down the paved trail. "Isn't it possible he had it with him in the plane?" Norm asked.

"I hadn't thought of that, but it is a possibility." I ran a little faster to keep up with his steady stride. "To tell you the truth, we both had the impression the nugget was worth a lot of money. I wouldn't expect Ken to carry it around in his pocket."

"It was definitely the envy of all the amateur gold seekers in our group. Pros too, for that matter. Anyway, after he found it, Ken figured he'd take his metal detector upstream and try to locate the source."

"Did he find it?"

"I think he found enough to stake a claim on a piece of open land, but I don't know the details. Last I talked to him, he was in the process of filing with the state."

That casts a whole new light on the subject. "Do you know where this claim is?"

"Not for sure," Norm said. "Ken was really close-mouthed about it. Didn't want word to spread before he concluded the legalities."

I glanced his way to see his expression. "Could you make an educated guess?"

"I could, but I won't. Ken didn't say, and it wouldn't do any good for me to speculate."

"It might help us find him if he went to the claim."

"No. I read the reports in the paper. He wasn't flying in that direction."

"Any clues you can give me would help. We're not having any luck finding him in the area he reported."

"I wish I could help," Norm said. "If I talk to anyone who knows more, I'll let you know."

I gazed out across the muddy waters of Cook Inlet, reluctant to turn back, but after glancing at my watch decided it was time. I thanked Norm and reversed course to return to my car. I thought about Ken's nugget and possible gold claim as I ran. Dad might be able to fill in some blanks for me. After all, he'd been leasing out his own gold claims near Nome for years.

The next morning, the weather was a clone of the day before. Rainy Pass weather was good, my social life not so much. It was too early to call Ross, so I left word for Angie to cancel my plans with him. Unfortunately, tenuous plans were one of the perils of living the life of a photo pilot.

The day's flight lines were complete by the time the sun angle started to fall. The job done, I returned to the hangar, stowed the guns in the safe and shipped the film for processing.

I checked my voice mail and listened to a message from a Larry Lindsey with the FAA. He was calling in response to the mislabeled part report I'd filed. It was unlikely he'd still be in the office so late in the day. I'd call him in the morning.

A package from Northern Airparts sat on my desk. Great. Dean would be happy to have at least one of the parts he needed. I removed the invoice, dropped it on Angie's desk and took the package to the hangar. Dean and Buzz were lying on the floor studying the twin's nose gear. Dean scrambled up when he saw me.

"I found this on my desk when I came in," I said. "Either Angie picked it up or they delivered it today." I handed him the package.

"Good," Dean said. "I need this. We'll get it installed tomorrow."

I left the office and drove downtown. While I had the time, I'd check a few jewelers and see what they could tell me about nugget values.

The first place I stopped didn't provide much help. The staff were inexperienced and did no custom nugget work. They referred me down the street to Bair's Nugget Jewelry.

The establishment was small with an older man peering through a lighted magnifying glass at something on his counter. Locked glass display cases lined the walls.

"Hello. Mr. Bair?" I asked as I moved towards him.

"Yes. Call me Griz. Everyone does. What can I do for you?"

I explained my mission. "I'm trying to determine an approximate value for a nugget weighing about five troy ounces. A friend of mine found it recently and now it's missing."

"Do you have a photograph?"

"Just on video, but I can give you a description…it's shape resembles the state of Indiana."

He nodded. "Oh, I think I've seen it. A fellow came in for an appraisal not long ago. Said he needed to insure it."

"Was his name Ken Abbott?"

"No, I don't think so. It was a name I associated with the movies. Let me think." He scratched his chin, then smiled. "Nico! Doesn't that sound like a good name for an actor?"

Not losing sight of the reason I was there, I continued with my questioning. "Do you remember what you told him it was worth?"

"I didn't appraise it. I offered to buy it, but he said it wasn't for sale right then."

"Do you recall the date he was in?"

"Sometime in the middle of the month. I'd just paid my mid-month bills and knew how much I could afford to offer."

"How much was that? Ballpark figure."

"I'd rather not say. You should ask him."

Frustrated, I returned to my office to check the address of Ken's apartment. I knew Nico had been out of town, but maybe he'd returned by now. I decided to close up for the day and swing by to see if he was home. As I gathered my things, I heard the outside hangar door close and Dean rev up his Harley Sportster. I glanced at the clock. Quitting time, but early for Dean to leave. He was usually the last one out.

The phone rang. It was my friend Kaitlin from the Ninety-Nines group. "Your cell phone must be turned off. Hope you don't mind my calling you at work."

"Not at all. I'm glad you did. I was so sad to hear your plane was stolen. Have you heard anything new?"

"Nothing yet. I'm afraid I'll never see it again, but I wanted to give you a description just in case. It's a Super Cub. White with blue trim."

By the time she'd finished telling me all the details and said good-bye, another fifteen minutes had passed, and I hurried to lock the doors and leave. I walked outside to the Subaru and noticed Buzz' green Toyota parked outside the hangar. That was odd. He should have left by now. Maybe a friend picked him up.

As I turned my key in the ignition, I heard two loud pops. At first I thought the noise came from my car, but realized it hadn't when the tires of a white SUV squealed as it sped off from the direction of the hangar. I'd heard gunshots.

Who would be shooting near the airplanes? I jumped out to see if there was any damage done and spotted a body lying on the tarmac outside the hangar. Dean's motorcycle lay nearby, its tires spinning. I ran.

"Dean!"

I knelt beside him and lifted the visor on his helmet. The face staring back at me was not Dean, but Buzz. He blinked and moved his mouth soundlessly. Blood streamed from one side of his face. I hit 9-1-1 on my phone and felt for his pulse with my free hand. The hangar door opened. Dean ran up as I told the dispatcher what few details I could about Buzz's condition.

"Buzz, can you hear me?" Dean shouted. "Hang in there, man. Help is on the way."

"We're right here with you, Buzz. You'll be okay." I prayed he would be and spread my jacket over him. It didn't stop his shivering, and his pulse seemed weak.

I turned to Dean. "I heard your Harley so I thought it was you."

"Buzz borrowed my bike. He wanted to try it out. I let him take it to Home Depot to pick up a clamp we needed." Dean's voice broke. "He must have been returning when it happened."

Flashing lights turned into the airport. Moments later, a stream of police cars blazed onto the tarmac. A group of officers surveyed the area for possible gunmen, while two approached us. The shorter patrolman, notebook in hand took a look at Buzz, winced, and asked if we'd witnessed what happened.

"I only heard it," I said, "but I did see a vehicle speed away immediately afterward." I bent down to adjust the jacket I'd placed over Buzz. "Please, get someone to help him."

"The paramedics are arriving now. Meanwhile, I need you to stand away from him. Can you give us a description of this vehicle?" the officer asked.

"An older model white SUV, but I didn't get the license plate." I thought for a moment. "I did see an orange sticker on the lower left corner of the rear window. I couldn't read what it said."

"Did you see who was inside?"

"I'm afraid not. I just got a glimpse of it."

"I didn't see the car," Dean said. "By the time I got the hangar door open, it was gone."

I waved to the paramedics and a fire truck parked some distance away. "Please hurry! He's in bad shape."

"They'll do their best for him," the taller officer reassured me. "They couldn't come in until the scene was cleared." He flipped a page in his notebook and started grilling us about any enemies Buzz might have. We both shook our heads.

"They may have meant to shoot me," Dean said.

The officer jerked his eyes to Dean's face. "Why would you think that?"

"He was wearing my helmet and riding my bike," Dean said.

"Any other reason?"

"Not that I can think of."

"How about you, Miss?" the officer asked.

"I can't imagine why anyone would want to shoot either of them. Buzz is a sweet kid and Dean gets along with everybody."

The paramedics loaded Buzz into an ambulance and took off. Alaska Regional Hospital was less than a half mile away. We had reason to hope they would make it there in time.

Dean held me close, his arm around my waist. We both shivered in shock, speechless while officers tied crime scene tape outside the hangar. I said a silent prayer for Buzz, not knowing what else I could do.

My thoughts were interrupted when the officer tapped my arm. "Miss, are you the victim's employer?"

"Yes."

"I'll need emergency contact information for him."

"Sure. I'll go inside to get it." I walked to the office door, unlocked it, and the officer followed me.

"No one in here when the shooting happened?"

"No. I was the last one out of the office. The information is inside the file cabinet." The officer pulled open the drawer I indicated. I grabbed the personnel file and copied Buzz's parents name, out-of-state address and phone number for the officer. "Can we go to the hospital now? I've told you all I know."

"We can continue this tomorrow downtown. We'll need a recorded statement. Meanwhile, if you think of any additional details, please give me a call." He handed me his card and followed me outside.

I reached for my cell phone, called the hospital, and left my name and cell number as a local emergency contact for Buzz. I relocked the office door and located Dean. We notified the police of our plan and jumped in my car for the five-minute drive to the hospital.

It was almost eight o'clock by the time Dean and I pulled into the emergency room parking lot. Located a block southeast of Merrill Field, the hospital is a low-profile building, just five stories high, built into a depression that was once part of the city landfill. It doesn't pose much of an aviation hazard, but until now it had always seemed like a strange place to build a hospital. Tonight, it seemed the perfect choice.

I identified myself at the nurse's station and asked about Buzz's condition.

"He's in surgery," the nurse said. "We'll let you know when he's out."

We checked in with the waiting room desk, found a couple of empty chairs and sat down to wait. I pulled out my phone and called Dad and Angie to let them know what was going on.

Before long, a nurse came over and directed us to a small room several doors down from the waiting area.

"You can wait here. Someone will be right in."

A few minutes later, the door opened.

"Hello. I'm the surgeon, Dr. Sprague," he said holding out his hand. "And you are…

I jumped up. "How is he?" I asked before he could continue.

"You're family?"

"No, I'm Beri Quinn, Buzz's employer, and this is Dean George, his supervisor. The shooting happened at my business. His parents live in Wyoming."

"We'll need to notify them right away. I'm very sorry, but I'm afraid his injuries were too extensive. He didn't survive long enough for us to help him. He barely made it to the operating room." The doctor placed a hand on my shoulder. "I've already informed the police officer who came in with him."

I sank back into my chair in disbelief. *This couldn't be happening.*

Dean didn't say a word, but after a few minutes he gave me his hand to pull me up.

"Thanks," I said. "Let's get out of here. I can't breathe."

We left the hospital, and I dropped Dean off at his condo, since his motorcycle was still part of the crime scene. "Be careful, Dean. Someone may try again if you were the one they were targeting."

I started home, tears streaming down my face, as I mulled over the awful events of the evening. I stopped the car and sat at the side of the road until I could see well enough to drive. Nineteen years old. Buzz was only nineteen years old. Who would want to kill him? But it didn't make any sense to think anyone would want to kill Dean, either.

Chapter Eleven

The next morning after returning from the police station, I sat at my desk and tried to divert my thoughts from the horrors of the day before. Not much work was being accomplished today. The skies were gray and cloudy. Grief and gloom pervaded the atmosphere of the office.

I called Buzz's parents, offered my condolences and learned they were making the arrangements to bring Buzz home to Wyoming as soon as his body was released. The police still had their crime scene tape surrounding the area outside the hangar. Buzz's Toyota and Dean's Harley had been towed off, but not much else had changed from the night before. I suggested everyone take the day off and go home, but no one did. We took solace from being together.

I thought of my conversation with Norm Underwood about Ken filing a claim. No wonder Ken didn't want to reveal where he'd found his nugget when asked by the television interviewer. I picked up the phone and called the Department of Mines and asked how I could find out if an individual had recently filed a gold claim. The official told me he couldn't release that information, but if I knew the location or the timeline of the filing I could search their records online. He warned me, however, that there was usually a lag of several months in posting the filings.

It was easy to pull up the website, but sure enough, the last posted entry was six months ago. Maybe Shawna could give me the location of the site. I sent her an e-mail and asked her to call me.

I scanned the website for locations near Rainy Pass, but I didn't come up with anything promising.

Dean poked his head in the office door. "Beri, I need you. The FAA inspector is here."

"Sure thing." I got up and walked out to the hangar, anxious to get to the bottom of our parts problem. "When did he arrive?"

"He was here waiting for me when I walked in a few minutes ago."

A large man with longish blond hair curling over the collar of his shirt stood in front of Dean's worktable, checking out the tools scattered there. The man was attractive in a ruddy-cheeked sort of way.

"Hello," he said, holding out his hand. "I'm Larry Lindsey. I need to ask a few questions about your report."

"Glad to meet you," I said and shook his hand. His grip was strong and lasted too long.

"Heard you had a shooting here last night," Lindsey said.

"Yes. A terrible thing." I looked down as tears started to well up in my eyes. "The police are investigating."

"Back to why I'm here," Lindsey said. "Your report says you've had a problem with misrepresented parts?"

"I asked for and purchased a new mag. The one I was given was packaged as new. After I delivered it to Dean, he came to me with concerns about it."

"When I removed it from the box to install it," Dean said, "it wasn't what was represented on the label. The data plate looked like it had been replaced, and the overall finish was worn. It was in worse shape than the old one I was trying to replace."

Lindsey turned to me. "You're sure you were told it was new?"

"Of course. That's what I asked for, and that's what the box indicated," I answered.

"I'd like to examine both the mag and the box," Lindsey said.

"Sure, they're over here," Dean said, rummaging through the contents of his workbench.

He moved rags, air filters and finally a case of oil. "That's weird. The mag is here, but the box isn't. I know I left the box right here behind my grinder, but it's gone now."

"That's too bad. Suspected unapproved parts or SUPS as we call them, are a big problem right now. The box would be helpful as evidence. Give me a call if it turns up," Lindsey said and turned to leave. "Thanks for the information. I'll be in touch after I've had time to check into this."

After Lindsey left, Dean muttered to himself. "Where could that box be?"

"Did the police search in here?" I asked.

"No. They left everything inside alone."

"Have you locked up when you've left during the day?"

"No, Angie is usually in the office and either Buzz or I are here. We alternated our breaks. Besides, I saw it this morning when I used the grinder."

"Strange."

"I did make a quick trip to the hardware store this morning, but wasn't gone more than fifteen minutes."

"That might be the answer," I said. "Anyone, including Hanratty himself, could have slipped in and taken the box while you were gone."

"I guess it's not that big a deal," Dean said.

"No, but it's enough that we're changing parts suppliers, and we'll start keeping the hangar door locked when you're gone."

Angie poked her head into the hangar and called to me. "Paige is on the line for you, Beri."

"Thanks." I walked inside to my desk and picked up the phone. "Hello, Paige. Good news, one more day of good weather and we'll complete the job."

"Let me know if I can help," Paige said.

"Sure will. I'll call you when conditions are right to finish. The forecast is good for tomorrow, but we'll have to see. Glad you're in town."

I disconnected and called the police to see if they could release our planes. The detective in charge agreed that the crime didn't appear to involve them and approved my request.

The next day I contacted Paige again to tell her the weather forecast was clear, and we could fly. While I had her on the phone, I asked if she'd been in contact with Nico.

"No," she said. "He's gone for the summer, and unfortunately I didn't get a contact number."

"How soon can you get here?"

"Give me fifteen minutes."

As soon as she arrived, we climbed in the plane and followed Ken's flight path one more time.

"This will be the day we find him," Paige said. "I can feel it."

"I hope you're right."

We entered the pass and flew in silence for several minutes. Sunlight glistened off rivulets of water dripping down the rocky creases from remnants of old snow melting higher up. I shifted in my seat and sighed. I knew it wouldn't be long before fresh snow fell in these mountains.

Paige sat in the rear seat of the Cub today and turned her head from one side window to the other scanning for Ken's plane.

"Why are so many airplanes painted white?" Paige asked. "You can't see them when it snows. You'd think that would be the last color you'd want in Alaska."

Even in August, random snow patches in protected areas served as potential camouflage for pieces of white wreckage.

"It does seem odd, but I think it's because a white exterior reflects heat and helps keep the plane cool," I said. "Also, the fabric doesn't deteriorate as fast."

"Hey, I think I saw something."

"Where?"

"Just below that cut we just passed. It looked like part of a wing. Can we go back?"

"Not yet. It's too narrow to turn around here. Check for landmarks, and we'll return later. I'll save the GPS coordinates of our position."

"It could have been snow, but I don't think so," Paige said. "When can we turn around?"

"Once we get the rest of the way through the pass, and since we have to go that far, I'll continue on to McGrath to get gas for the trip back to Anchorage. Meanwhile, we'll finish taking pictures."

By the time we reached McGrath and refueled, high stratus clouds appeared around the edges of the mountains on the west side. Visibility was still good, although the ceiling was lower.

"A warm front may be heading this way," I said. "If we return now, we should be okay."

"Let's go. I'm anxious to get another look at what I saw."

We climbed into our seats and started back through the pass. I turned to talk to Paige. "Pay special attention to any remnant of tail numbers. That's the first thing CAP will ask for."

"I'll give it my best shot," Paige said. "All I remember seeing was part of a wing. I don't think there were any numbers."

I focused ahead. "We're getting close. I'll let you know when we reach the coordinates. Should be in just a few minutes."

"Search for a cleft where the rock is fossilized on the far side."

"Fossilized?"

"Mmmhmm. The color is different, lighter."

"That may help. We're coming up on it now. Stay sharp."

"See it?" Paige pointed to a spot almost halfway down a deep slash in the rock face. "It *is* a wing. It's right there!"

"I saw it. Can't really identify it, but I'll call it in to see if there's any record of a crash here." I turned the dials on the radio and punched in the CAP frequency. I hoped it wasn't Ken's plane. Not much chance of surviving a crash this high in the pass.

CAP radioed to me that they had no record of a wrecked plane at the location

I'd reported. They would send a team to check it out."

Paige tapped my shoulder. "What do you think?"

I shrugged in my seat. "I think the wingtip was too square for a Piper, but we'll have to wait and see."

"It's Ken's plane. I know it is, Beri." Paige twisted a tissue in her hand into a tight rope.

Possibly it was, but I didn't want our search to end this way. The rest of the trip continued without incident or conversation.

Once at Merrill, we taxied to the hangar, and I noticed that all signs of crime tape were gone. That was a relief. I paused on the taxiway and prayed the CAP report would find the plane we'd located wasn't Ken's. I couldn't bear the thought my worst fears would be confirmed.

Chapter Twelve

When I got home, Dad was sitting in his recliner with his feet up watching golf on television. He didn't play golf, but it was a sport so he was interested.

"Good to see you taking it easy, Dad. I could use a bit of that myself."

"Everything okay, cupcake?" He pressed the mute button on the remote.

"Yes." I sat on the arm of the sofa near him. "Still in shock, but functioning. A memorial service for Buzz is planned at the University next week."

Dad shook his head. "Hell of a thing. Who'd shoot a kid in cold blood?"

"At this point, the police don't have any clues. It doesn't help that there are so many white SUVs in this town."

He patted my arm. "Hang in there. It'll take time."

"There's something else you might be able to help me with. Where would someone be likely to file a gold claim in the McGrath area? Any good spots come to mind?"

"No idea. There are gold mines and creeks all over the place out there. Why?"

"Ken may have filed a claim shortly before he went missing, but I don't know where. I called the state mining office, but without a location or an exact date I drew a blank."

Dad took a swig of his beer. "Sorry, I can't help, but that reminds me. I scheduled my trip to collect my stake from my leased claims."

Jack walked in the room and overheard. "Where're you going, Gramps?"

"Up north to check my claims. My annual visit."

Jack tilted his face to the side. "Did you find your claims during the gold rush? We studied it in Alaska history last year."

"I'm not quite that old. No, I got them the easy way."

"How's that?" Jack asked.

"I inherited them."

"Really? Who from? Tell me more."

"My Great Uncle Sanford. He spent years prospecting in Alaska. Made and lost several fortunes in his lifetime, but never married. I was overseas in the military when he died and left his remaining claims to his nephews. I've leased mine out and kept the assessments current ever since." Dad clicked the volume button on his remote.

"When do you leave?" I asked.

"The Jeters had a good year so I'm anxious to get up there. I made reservations for next week."

"Wish I could go with you," Jack said. "I've never seen a gold mine."

"Maybe I can take you sometime, but there's not a lot to see. Just a creek and a dredge. Not much space for visitors, either. The Jeters live in a small cabin. I sleep in my tent and spend most of my nights swatting mosquitos. Besides, it's a long walk on muskeg to get there. It's a balancing act. You walk from clump to clump of mossy unstable ground. The mounds are so shaky, you're afraid you're going to slip off into the water surrounding them and twist an ankle."

Jack smiled. "I'll bet the birding is super up near Nome though."

"Yes. You'd probably like that part. If you think you can handle the rest of it, we can plan a trip together someday, but not this year. My travel arrangements are set and you've got your baseball tournament to get ready for."

"I'm not going to be here for the tournament anyway, remember? I'm going to visit my dad."

Frank bent down to stare directly in Jack's face. "Now listen to me young man, you made a commitment to your team to play. That's the same as giving your word. You ask your dad to schedule your trip so you don't miss it."

Jack's chin jutted out. "I'm going no matter what. Besides, I suck at baseball. The team doesn't even want me."

"Jack, don't talk to your grandfather that way. I'm sure we can figure out a schedule that works for everybody." I frowned at Dad. "We'll plan on Jack going to Nome next year if you two think you can get along well enough to spend a few days traveling together."

Both of the men in my life rolled their eyes at me and turned away.

Chapter Thirteen

Paige arrived at the office early the next morning, her eyes swollen. She looked at me with a combination of hope and fear. "Have you heard anything about the plane we found?"

"Sorry, not yet. We should hear soon." I handed her a disc "You can help search through the first batch of processed pictures. They should help keep your mind occupied while we wait."

The contrast and clarity of the photos allowed us to scan much more territory than our two sets of eyes had been able to from the plane. But there were so many of them.

My phone rang after I'd worked for about an hour. The police detective wanted Dean and me to stop by the police station and complete our statements. I agreed that we'd be there later in the day.

The phone continued to interrupt me all morning. Each time it rang, Paige flinched. I took time to peruse the stack of mail Angie handed me. Bills and advertisements predominated, but there was an envelope from Cartos. I tore it open hoping it was a new sub-contracting job. Instead, it was a note confirming our plans for the gala and giving me the particulars. Black tie, optional. Oh my. I hoped my wardrobe would be up to the challenge.

Paige continued without a break until noon. "Whew. Quite a process," she said finally. "We better turn up something after all this effort."

"We're only viewing our coverage of the southeast end now," I said. "The probability we'll find something will increase the farther we get into the pass."

"That's good. We don't have those pictures yet though, do we?"

"No, I just sent them in for processing."

"Well, I think I'll break for a bit and get some lunch. I'll be back soon."

After Paige left, I got the call I'd been waiting for—CAP with an update on the crashed plane we'd spotted.

"What did you find?" I asked.

"The terrain is dangerous around the site, and we haven't reached it on foot yet. We have determined by helicopter that the plane is a Maule M-9-235. It's not the one you were searching for, but we're glad you located it. We're in the process of notifying the family that it's been found."

I clicked the phone off and let out the breath I'd been holding, relieved that it hadn't been Ken's plane. Paige should be happy, too. Under the circumstances, uncertainty trumped certain death. I made a quick call and gave her the news.

I decided to follow Paige's lead and grab a bite to eat. I walked out to the hangar to tell Dean I was leaving and found him deep in conversation with Ross. I hadn't realized they were acquainted.

"Hello. This is a surprise," I said.

"Couldn't help but notice all your planes are parked. Since you're not flying, how about joining me for lunch?" Ross said.

"Good idea. I was just leaving."

Ross opened the door to his Jeep. "Hop in."

I glanced at him. He appeared as fit and confident as ever, but his eyes didn't squint with their usual sense of amusement. He looked tired.

Ross opened the driver's door and slid in. "How does Arctic Roadrunner sound?"

"Delicious. Haven't had one of their burgers in a long time."

We drove in uncomfortable silence for several minutes as Ross turned south.

"I didn't realize you knew Dean," I said. "Seems like everyone associated with aviation in this town knows everyone else."

Ross glanced my way. "Dean and my mechanic are friends. That's how we met, but I don't know him well. I hear he's a crackerjack mechanic."

"You've got that right. I couldn't manage without him."

Ross pulled into the parking lot, and we went inside.

"Why don't you snag a table outside by the creek while I get the food?" Ross took a place in line. "You still a Kenai Whopper gal?"

"Sure, with a diet Coke, please."

The juicy burger with a zing of jalapenos brought back a flurry of memories. Ross and I had downed many of them when we were dating. Before Dennis. Before a lot of things.

We were halfway through our burgers before Ross started to tell me why he wanted to see me. I sat up straighter, returned to the present and let the memories fade away.

"The reason I wanted to meet for lunch is to explain why I acted like such a fool after the CAP search session." He hunched his shoulders forward and placed his hand on my arm. "It's embarrassing. I was angry because I thought you were responsible for some problems I've been having."

"Problems? Really?"

"Yeah. Someone's been bad-mouthing my business. I've been losing customers over it. Since you're my main competitor, I assumed it had to be you." He shook his head. "Stupid. I know you better than that."

"I'm glad you came to your senses," I said. "Of course, I'd never try to discredit you, and I can't imagine who would."

"I know, I know."

"What's been happening?"

Ross gazed out over Campbell Creek bordering the terrace of the restaurant and sighed. "Lots of cancellations. All with vague reasons. One fellow said it was because I had a terrible safety record. When I denied it and asked where he'd heard it, he shrugged and said the word was out."

"So rumors, then?"

"Mostly, although I've also had a rash of weird mechanical problems. Nothing my mechanic can't handle, but it's odd how I've had such a cluster of them. And a few of my students have been behaving irrationally."

"Irrationally. How so?"

"For example, I took one student out last week and on our return, he headed into a controlled area. He ignored my instructions to contact air traffic control and entered traffic opposite to the designated direction. I demanded he turn around, but the dumb ass ignored me. I had to physically take over the controls and correct the approach."

"Wow!" I said. "I'm sure air traffic control wasn't happy about that."

"Not at all. Of course they faulted me as the instructor. I had the strong sense the fellow intended that all along. It was all I could do to keep from decking him."

"So what do you think is behind all this?"

Ross stared at a distant spot. "Who knows? Maybe someone's trying to ruin me. I've been nosing around trying to find out who it is. My best guess is it's someone who wants to take over my space on Merrill Field. There's a long waiting list to lease space from the Municipality. Maybe they figure they'll speed up the process if they can push some of the smaller operators out. They're getting damn close to succeeding with me."

"Has anyone approached you about taking over your lease?"

"Not directly, no, but my lease doesn't work that way. If I leave, the lease reverts to the city. Applications for the space would go through the Municipality."

"I'd better check mine. Dad negotiated it years ago, and I haven't paid much attention to it, except to make payments."

"Good idea. Because if I'm right about this—you could be next, Beri."

Chapter Fourteen

I slammed the file drawer closed in frustration. I couldn't find a copy of our lease.

Shawna saved me from completely losing my temper when she came through the office door balancing a bakery box in her hands. "Hello folks. I got in from Juneau last night and brought nourishment—wild blueberry scones."

"Smells wonderful," I said. "Good to see you."

"I was glad to get your e-mail. I've been wishing I could do something to help with the investigation." She set the box down on my desk. "I know Ken planned to file a claim, but I don't know exactly where. I'd guess somewhere near his recent prospecting site."

"Can you help me find it?"

"I think so. When can we get started?"

"Today's good. You know Ken's habits better than anybody so let's find where you think he'd go." I motioned to the wall.

Shawna pinpointed an area east of Lake Iliamna on the wall map. "It's somewhere near here."

"Nowhere near Rainy Pass."

"That's what I've been trying to tell everyone. I don't care about his flight plan, this is where he said he was going."

"Okay, we'll check it out. Have a seat and catch up with Angie while I file a flight plan and pre-flight the 180." I stopped mid-stride. "Oh, and Angie, would you dig out our lease agreement from the filing cabinet? I tried to find it, but didn't finish the job before Shawna arrived."

I walked outside, freed the plane from its tie-downs and started through my checklist. When I got to the fuel check, I drained a little gas from each side to make sure water hadn't condensed in the tanks. I checked to make sure the color in the strainer tube was a consistent blue color without any bubbles.

When I went inside to get Shawna, I grabbed emergency gear and maps for the trip. Shawna waved good-bye to Angie and followed me out to the plane. She talked non-stop until she buckled herself into her seat and then fell silent.

After take-off, the sound of the engine exhaust and the prop coalesced into a duet of white-noise, partially, but not completely muffled by our headsets.

Shawna appeared nervous in the plane, chattering in spurts about Ken. "I'll never forget the time he took me moose hunting," she said. "He and his roommate both killed their moose, and both animals had these huge racks. They were so big they didn't fit into either plane, but no way were the guys going to leave them behind." She laughed and fidgeted in her seat. "So what did they do? Ken strapped one set of antlers to each wing of his Cub and flew them out that way. I was in the other plane, and I was convinced it would never work, but Ken said he knew what he was doing, and apparently, he did. He's still got those antlers hanging in his living room."

"I hadn't heard Ken tell that story, but as long as he strapped them on upside down so the rounded edge faced up, it would be safe enough. I know it appears dramatic, but it's common practice for hunters flying Cubs."

We flew above the terrain of the Alaska Range and leveled out to head north of Port Alsworth.

"There!" Shawna said, pointing to Mesa Mountain. "I know we flew past here when we checked his claim."

I descended to 3000 feet. The airspeed indicator quivered, and the instrument panel rattled with an erratic vibration. Uh oh.

Shawna jerked sideways to stare at me. "Is that normal?"

I shook my head. I'd been flying using my left fuel tank. I quickly turned the fuel selector to access both tanks, turned on the auxiliary fuel pump and put the plane into a shallow bank. I scanned the terrain below for potential landing sites along the river. Not much improvement in the plane's performance. The prop rattled. The plane jerked. The engine quit completely.

Silence except for wind noise.

I grabbed the radio, dialed 121.5 and called mayday! "Mayday, mayday! This is 3868 Foxtrot. Engine failure. I'm approximately 200 miles northwest of Anchorage and south of Chilikadrotna River."

"Roger that, 3868 Foxtr…"

Did he get our location or not? He did say "roger" before his transmission conked out. I tried again, but the radio failed to key when I clicked the mic.

Shawna's eyes widened. She clutched the armrests, nails digging into the surface.

I focused on landing the plane. The sandbars on the river were too small for an attempt, and I wasn't excited about being stranded in the middle of the river if the water was deep. I determined the wind direction by checking the direction of the ripples on a small lake below. The water was smooth adjacent to the beach on the north side, and the birds on the water were all facing the same way, so I figured I'd better land to the north to be into the wind.

Spotting an area of dry swamp that appeared to be covered only in tall grass, I flipped the master switch and magnetos off, and popped both doors.

"Hold on!" I said, and brought the plane down.

We heard the grass swish against the belly of the plane, followed by a heart-stopping THUNK!

The plane flipped.

We found ourselves hanging upside down in our seats as the plane skidded along on its roof. When we finally stopped, I twisted to my right feeling like I was hanging from a trapeze.

"Shawna, Shawna, are you all right?"

"I think so. Except for my arm. It must have hit something."

"We need to get out. Now!"

Bracing myself against one arm of my seat, I pushed against the side wall with my legs while undoing my seatbelt. I managed to control my drop to the ceiling without landing on my head and turned to assist Shawna.

"Which arm is the problem?" I asked.

"The right one. I'm afraid to fall on it."

"I'll hold you so you don't." I grabbed her left shoulder. "Here goes." I released the latch on her belt.

She fell solidly against my chest, pushing me against the visors. The smell of aviation fuel was beginning to permeate the cabin. I realized my knees were wet with the stuff.

"Get out. Hurry! Brace your back against mine. We'll push on the doors with our legs. Here goes. One, two, three, *push.*"

Shawna's door opened. Mine didn't budge. "Quick, see if you can crawl out."

Shawna bent double and holding her injured arm with her good hand, squeezed out of the plane and onto the wing.

"I'm right behind you. Run as far away from the tail as you can in case fire breaks out in the engine."

I paused at the door of the plane before jumping out to see if I could spot any accessible survival gear, but saw nothing. A few minutes later, we sat on a small hillock, batting mosquitoes and staring down at the plane. No fire. Not yet anyway.

Shawna rocked herself back and forth. "What happened? Did we hit something?"

"Yeah. We hit a rock or a stump hidden in the grass. I'll explore later and find out exactly what it was." I knelt and put a hand on her shoulder. "How are you doing?"

"I'll live, if these dratted mosquitoes don't do me in."

I slipped out of my emergency flying vest. "They didn't put twenty-two pockets in this thing for nothing."

I yanked open a couple of Velcro flaps and pulled out mosquito head netting and packets of deet repellant. "Here, let me put one of these nets on you. Next, I'll take a peek at that arm."

Her forearm hung unnaturally in a subtle S shape. I had a few first-aid supplies in my vest, but most of them, including the splints were in my survival bag in the plane. I wasn't ready to go there yet.

"Are you in pain? I have some Tylenol if it would help."

"I'm okay," she said, teeth chattering.

"Don't go shocky on me." I pulled a space blanket out of a deep pocket. "I'll drape this around you to help keep you warm until I can build a fire."

I removed the PLV—Personal Locator Beacon—from my vest and activated it as a back-up to the emergency locator beacon in the plane. One thing I knew for sure, the sooner we were located and Shawna could get medical attention, the better. I whipped out my cell phone hoping to reach Dad before he heard about the accident on the news, but as usual when away from town, no bars appeared.

I stood and surveyed our surroundings. Lots of grass and black spruce. Some willow and alder along the river. Plenty of water. Shawna sat on a sandy rise with few rocks. Not a bad place for a shelter unless the wind became an issue. Judging from the clouds building behind the mountains, trouble with wind was a distinct possibility.

I broke off the lower branches of the black spruce trees around us. The lower branches are often dead and are almost always drier than the others. Fortunately, I didn't have to worry about setting the grass on fire, as it wasn't dry at all. Not much dries out during the summer in Alaska. Despite the moisture in the air, my military fire starter flared instantly.

Shawna hunched toward the small campfire I built as soon as it caught. When the plane's engine had cooled enough to check the plane for more supplies, I left her and hiked to the wreckage. The damage to the plane was almost total. It lay on its back with the body of the fuselage twisted grotesquely to the left. I peered in the open door to see what I could salvage and spotted our stainless steel thermos. *Lucky we weren't hit in the head with it.* I noticed the antenna was broken off the ELT. A couple of rolls of white pre-mark plastic rested on the plane's ceiling. It's used for making large X's on the ground to serve as control points for mapping photography. I grabbed them and placed them on the ground with the thermos.

I could see the survival bag now toward the rear and reached in to grab it. I pulled, but couldn't get a good grip. Part of the fuselage was wrapped around it, wedging it firmly in place. The cramped space prevented me from cutting into the bag to reach any of the contents. I tugged again and again and finally managed to pull loose an adjacent tarp. Unfortunately, almost all our food was trapped inside the duffle.

I returned to where Shawna waited. "Success or at least partial success." I displayed my bounty. "I managed to retrieve this much for now. I'll try again later."

After I poured her a cup of lukewarm coffee in the thermos lid, I stirred a package of instant cocoa from my vest into the coffee. "Your mocha is served. Almost as good as Starbucks."

She took the cup in her good hand. "You certainly came prepared. What else do you have in that vest of yours?"

"A little of this and a little of that. I've always believed in surviving in as much comfort as possible. Besides, chocolate is an absolute essential." I glanced up at the gathering clouds in the increasingly leaden sky. Rain was coming.

I pointed to a tree about fifty feet away with a branch large enough to support our tarp. "Think you can make it to that tree? It would make a good place to set up camp."

"As long as you promise to build another fire. I think that mocha gave me a little energy."

We trudged across the spongy grass together. I lugged the tarp and draped it over the branch. Shawna collapsed in a heap, leaning her back against the tree trunk.

It made what I hoped would be an adequate shelter, so I scavenged for more black spruce branches. It took most of my bundle to get another fire started. I hurried to whittle the last few into stakes to tie the tarp down so I could stash more firewood under the tarp before the rain came.

Luck was with me. I finished the job just before the rain hit. We huddled under the tarp to stay dry, breathing in the piney scent of the wood and spruce needles surrounding us. Shawna was holding her own, but I worried how she'd handle the chill as night came.

"More coffee?" I asked. "While it's still a little warm?"

"I'll share it with you," she said. "I think I'm ready for that Tylenol."

I pulled open a flap and handed her the pills. "Want to split a granola bar? I have a few more for later. I patted my vest pockets. "Another packet of cocoa in here, too."

"Ken always wore his vest when he flew in the bush, but I never checked the contents. What doesn't it have?"

"Lots of things, I'm afraid. Sleeping bags, for example. It's designed for situations like this when a pilot escapes his plane, but can't retrieve anything he isn't wearing."

"It's a magic vest. I'm so glad you wore it."

"I'll try to get the survival gear out of the plane again tomorrow. It's getting a good soaking with this rain so I won't have to worry quite as much about causing a fire."

We sat, listening to the pelting rain on the tarp. Thankfully, wind wasn't a big problem. Lulled, Shawna fell asleep sitting up. I tucked the space blanket snugly around her and sat thinking about Jack. I knew Dad would keep him safe, but I didn't want him worried about me. Not for the first time, I wished Alaska had better cell phone service. It worked well in Anchorage and Juneau, but not many other areas. Finally, I managed to doze into a fitful sleep.

"Beri! Do you hear that? What's making that noise?"

I awoke, startled. Darkness finally blotted out daylight. The rain had stopped, but a new kind of racket replaced it. I stood and stretched my stiff legs. A loud tearing sound came from the direction of the plane, punctuated by occasional whuffs and grunts. A bear!

"I'll go rebuild the fire, and see if I can see anything." I carried an armload of branches out to the circle of rocks that had contained our fire. It took a moment for the new wood to catch, but the flames grew steadily even in the moisture saturated air. I hoped the fire would keep the bear away from our shelter.

Under the tarp again, I pulled my head lamp from its pocket and handed it to Shawna. "The fire gives off a lot of light, but if we have to evacuate, this will help."

"Do you think bears will come after us?" I could tell she was scared.

"No, but it's good to be prepared."

"I don't hear them anymore," Shawna said. "That's a good thing, isn't it?"

"Sure. It's probably only one bear, and we'd hear it stomping through the brush if it came this way. The fire should help discourage it."

"Unless the bears are cold, too," Shawna said in a small voice.

Chapter Fifteen

The next morning, Shawna's skin was pale and clammy. She'd lost some of her spunk. I heated the last of the coffee in the thermos cap and stirred in the final cocoa packet.

"Here, drink this fast before any bears in the area smell it. And take a couple more Tylenol while you're at it."

"Thanks." She took the cup in her mittened left hand. "How long do you think it will be before they pick up our signal and come get us?"

"With this overcast, it's hard to say. Dean will be chomping at the bit to rescue us. They'll be here as soon as they can." I reached for more spruce branches. "I'll build up the fire and go see what happened down by the plane last night."

"You think it's safe?" Shawna asked.

"Sure. If it was a bear, it'll be long gone. I'll check things out and build an SOS signal to help rescuers spot us."

I ducked out from under the tarp and walked towards the plane. The dirt was damp under my boots. Ground fog drifted over the landscape. The temperature was about fifty degrees, not cold, but the moist air penetrated my clothing.

I spotted a paw print a few feet from the plane. The bear had shredded the entire passenger side of the fuselage to get into the rear cargo area. As I examined the damage, I saw that he'd managed to accomplish what I could not. He'd extricated the emergency supply bag and ripped it to shreds. Not a morsel of food remained. Even the hatchet handle had teeth marks. I salvaged the guns, ammo and what was left of the hatchet. The sleeping bags were ruined, although I gathered up the less tattered of the two to carry to camp. It would provide a little warmth. No sign of the medical supply kit.

Outside the plane, I found a fallen tree hidden in the grasses that I must have hit on landing. Six feet to the left, and I'd have missed it entirely.

When I returned to camp, I found Shawna snoring, still wrapped in the space blanket. I dumped everything except the pistol on the ground beside her, loaded the Smith & Wesson and carried it with me. A few minutes of rummaging inside the plane revealed a couple of tools that had been stored in the back of it.

Using the pliers, I removed the cotter pin holding one of the seats to the rail above my head. Only one bolt remained to hold the seat in place. I loosened it, carefully lowered the seat to my shoulders and carried it to camp.

Shawna moaned in her sleep. I set the aircraft seat beside her and lifted her onto the cushion. She'd stay a little warmer up off the ground. She didn't wake up which disturbed me. *Was she conscious?*

I knew it was critical to keep her warm. She wasn't wearing a hat so I fashioned a cocoon for her head from shredded sleeping bag insulation and piled the rest over her chest.

Time to mark out a ground-to-air distress signal to make our situation apparent to passing planes and searchers.

I grabbed the rolls of pre-mark plastic and cleared a flat stretch of river bank. Visibility was still too low to expect a search party, but we would be prepared when it lifted. I anchored the white strips with rocks and laid out a three foot by ten foot stripe on the flattest stretch of ground I could find. It was the signal for "need medical assistance-serious injury," an indicator printed on the back of every hunting license in Alaska.

Surveying my work, I sighed. Both the signal and the plane would be clearly visible from the air. A feathery mist of rain covered my face and lashes blurring my vision as I jogged to camp.

Shawna still slept, but the space blanket had slipped. I rearranged it, added a few more clumps of insulation and put more wood on the fire outside. I hoped the light rain wouldn't extinguish it.

I opened the thermos and poured river water I'd treated with purification tablets into a pouch I'd formed from a square of heavy-duty foil from my vest. Setting the pouch in the fire while the coals still burned, I heated it for some tea which was about all I had left in the way of rations.

The tea, brewed as strong as I could make it and fortified with several packets of sugar didn't help rouse Shawna. She barely stirred when I held it near her face hoping the steam would wake her. I held it to her lips anyway and forced a small amount between her lips. When she wouldn't take more, I finished the rest of the cup myself.

Even with the caffeine boost, I felt drowsy. I leaned against the remaining pile of firewood and dozed, dreaming of frying bacon and syrupy flapjacks. I awoke to find Shawna unchanged. I gathered my hatchet and gun and started for the river.

Chapter Sixteen

The surface of the water dimpled as fish surfaced to feast on the mosquitoes and no-see-ums hovering above. Fish were plentiful, but could I catch one? I climbed up the bank until I found a willow branch I could fashion into a pole. Hacking at it with my hatchet, I skinned the branch of twigs and leaves until I created an eight-foot Huckleberry Finn-type pole.

I notched the tip, tied fishing line in a slip knot with two half-hitches behind it and hoped it would hold the monster fish I'd catch. I added a mosquito fly from my vest, and using the best fly-fishing technique I could muster, I whipped it out into the water.

No soap. It landed about a yard from my feet still on the bank. My second attempt hooked an alder branch behind me.

Gathering up a lariat of line to shorten my cast, I flipped the fly out underhand into the current and gradually let it out. This approach appeared more promising, but an hour later I hadn't had a nibble.

I spotted about a dozen ptarmigan clustered downstream from me. Next trip, I'm bringing a shotgun. My large caliber pistol would transform a bird into mincemeat and feathers. Or, maybe not.

Taking careful aim at a pile of rocks just ahead of the covey of birds, I pulled the trigger. Rock chips sprayed and two ptarmigans fell and lay unmoving on the bank. Several of the other birds flew away, but the rest rushed over to their dead peers to see what happened. I figured I could take them out the same way, but two birds would be enough for now. I walked over to pick up dinner, finally scaring the rest away.

It took a few minutes to clean the ptarmigan and toss the innards in the water for the fish. When finished, I picked up my pole and pulled my line to shore. I felt a tug, gentle at first, but stronger as I pulled more line. I'd caught something after all. A grayling, dorsal fin fanning above its back like a small sailfish hung from my hook.

Fish and fowl. We'd have a feast. I only hoped Shawna would wake up long enough to eat. I cleaned the grayling and gathered more spruce branches, deciding to rebuild our original fire near the plane instead of cooking in camp. I didn't want to encourage a visit to our camp from a bear while we slept.

The fish cooked quickly in a foil packet placed in the coals. I left the ptarmigan roasting slowly on a spit of green alder branches while I encouraged Shawna to eat a few bites of grayling. She stirred slightly, but turned away from the food. I forced a few sips of sweetened tea between her lips and felt her throat for a pulse. Her skin was damp with perspiration, and her pulse felt fast and thready. Shawna was in real trouble.

It was time to scavenge more firewood to build up the fire. I managed to gather an armload and replenished the fire near the shelter. Shawna might be sweaty, but she needed to stay warm. I went back to the plane, surveying the sky. The ground fog had lifted a bit. Good news, I hoped. I sat by my cooking fire and ate the grayling. The aroma from the sizzling ptarmigan made me think of turkey roasting and Thanksgivings past. The last time I'd seen my mother was the Thanksgiving when I was five. She'd left the next morning. I hoped Jack realized I'd never do that to him.

As I removed the ptarmigan from the fire, I heard the whup, whup of a helicopter reverberate through the air. I jumped to my feet waving my skewered birds to attract attention. I watched as the military chopper hovered, searching for a clearing to land. It slowed and settled about a hundred yards from the crashed plane, flattening the grass with its rotor wash.

The door slid open and two rescuers jumped out. "Anybody hurt?" the taller one yelled above the noise.

Relief flooded through me—we were saved. My legs went wobbly for a moment before I took off at a run.

"Yes. This way!" I led them toward our shelter.

"Broken arm," I shouted. "Maybe internal injuries or hypothermia." I slowed as we reached the camp.

The medics moved Shawna to a stretcher, carried her back and loaded her into the chopper. I put out our fire and followed behind with my lucky thermos, tarp and weapons in tow.

"You okay?" one of the men yelled to me.

I nodded and he gave me a hand up into the chopper.

"Let's get this buggy in the air."

We were airborne within minutes.

The chopper landed smoothly at the Providence Hospital helipad, and the medics unloaded Shawna, an IV already dripping into her veins.

The pilot motioned me over before I stepped down out of the chopper. "The guys think she'll be okay. Good thing we got her here when we did."

"Thanks," I said, wiping away tears. "I'm glad she'll be okay."

"Say, what did you do with those birds you were waving around?"

"The ptarmigan? I guess I left them on board somewhere."

"I'll see if I can find them. They smelled delicious."

I laughed for the first time all day. "They're all yours."

Chapter Seventeen

Dad and Jack met me at the hospital and Jack rushed into my arms. After a big hug, he stepped back with a sober expression and slowly surveyed me from head to foot.

"I'm fine, Jack. Really. I'm okay, and I'm so glad to see you!"

"Mom. We were so worried." He brushed tears from his eyes. "What happened to you anyway?"

"I couldn't get back because we had a problem with the airplane and made an emergency landing. The plane's banged up, and Shawna broke her arm, but everything will be all right."

Dad patted me on the back. "So, you got to practice some of those wilderness survival techniques you preach about all the time, eh?"

"You betcha. The training helped a lot." I sighed. "What do you say we go home? I can't wait for a hot shower and maybe some of your pancakes."

"It's a deal. I have a new batch of sourdough starter I want to try out."

Shawna left the hospital the following day. She called to tell me that she planned to recuperate for a few days at a friend's apartment before returning to Juneau. I drove to the address she gave me off C Street, which turned out to be a large complex of identical condominiums. After circling the parking lot a couple of times, I found the unit number and a parking space not marked "reserved". I grabbed the box of cookies I'd baked for her and walked to the unit on the far end.

Disco music rumbled from inside. I rang the bell and was surprised when Shawna answered the door herself, her face flushed. How she heard the bell over the noise was a mystery to me. She wore sweats and a baggy "Grown in Alaska" tee-shirt with one sleeve cut out. Her arm, in a cast, hung in a sling through the opening.

"Beri. Just a sec. I'll turn the music down." She adjusted the volume and returned to close the door behind me. "Good of you to come."

"Wow. I didn't expect to see you feeling so energetic already. Your doctor's okay with working out?"

"Not a problem as long as I don't jolt the arm. A little exercise is a good thing. Definitely better than lying around in that hospital bed another day." She moved some magazines from the sofa. "Here, sit so we can talk. I'm ready for a break."

I set the box of cookies on the table. "These are for you. Jack insisted I make you his favorite oatmeal raisin. I think he had an ulterior motive."

"Thanks. Tell him they're my favorite, too." She fiddled with the edge of her cast and cleared her throat. "Uh, Beri? There's something you might want to know."

I tilted my head to the side. "What's that?"

"A couple of investigators interviewed me before I was discharged from the hospital. I hope I didn't say anything that will cause you trouble." Her voice dropped lower. "I didn't mean to anyway."

"Who were they?" I asked.

"FAA, I think. I answered their questions, but I don't know much about flying rules, so I hope I answered right."

"What did they ask you?"

Shawna shrugged, then winced. "Oh, did you appear intoxicated or incapacitated in any way, did you follow basic safety rules, things like that."

"Sounds routine. What did you say?"

"I told them you staggered out to the plane and reeked of alcohol." She laughed. "No, of course not, I told them you were perfectly sober and we survived because you were such a good pilot."

"Thanks for the vote of confidence. Did they ask anything else?"

"Just questions about how you decided where to land, and what the engine sounded like. Was it on or did you switch it off? Those kinds of questions worried me. It's such a blur in my mind, I wasn't sure what to say."

"All you could do was tell them what you remembered. Don't worry about it. I can fill in any details they need. Thanks for letting me know. I'm glad you're doing better. You had me worried."

"Sorry about that. I'm sure glad to be home." She stood, and shifted from one foot to the other. "Will you return that way again soon—to search for Ken's plane?"

"Of course. As soon as weather permits. I'm not giving up on him."

During the drive to the office, I puzzled over my next step. I'd fly out to the sites Shawna had marked on the map before our ill-fated trip. It still didn't make sense that Ken would file his flight plan one way if he planned to go somewhere else. Why would he do that? I needed to check the flight plan myself.

Back in my office, I found our lease agreement sitting on my desk. I paged through it as I picked up the phone and called the Flight Service Station to ask how I could get access to the recording of Ken's flight plan.

"I want to listen to the tape," I told the staffer. "It's my plane that's missing, and I need to figure out what happened."

"All tapes more than a week old are archived off-site. Besides, they're not available to the public."

"But can't you make an exception? We're trying to save a man's life here."

"Nothing I can do, he replied."

My efforts to convince him otherwise completely unsuccessful, I slammed down the phone in disgust. At that moment, Ross walked into the office.

"I hate unreasonable people," I grumbled.

"Who's so unreasonable?" Ross sat down across from me.

"Flight Service. I need to listen to the tape of Ken's flight plan, but they aren't cooperating."

"They have the tapes?"

"Apparently. Archived but not available to the public."

"Probably depends on who you talk to," Ross said.

"What do you mean?"

"Like with most everything, it helps to have friends in the right places."

"You know somebody?" I leaned closer. "Who?"

Ross smiled a slow smile and shook his head. "Not so fast. We'll need to discuss this. How about I pick you up at six?"

"Come on, Ross. That sounds too much like a date. Those days are behind us."

He laughed. "Do you want my help or not?"

The doorbell rang a few minutes before six. Dad closed his newspaper. He'd delayed his trip to Nome after the Jeters called to say they'd come down with the flu. He seemed extremely interested that I had a gentleman caller and asked for details about our plans.

"It's Ross McEvoy," I said. "I'm not sure where we're going. We need to talk about business."

"Ross? I always liked that boy. Never did understand why you ditched him for Dennis back in the day." He motioned me forward. "Well, get on with it. Open the door and let the poor guy in."

"You're early," I said to Ross as he stood on the front step. He'd changed from his work clothes into a close-fitting Henley that accentuated his muscular shoulders. He looked good. *Too good.* Better watch it, or I'd have another complication in my life. One I didn't need.

"Since you're ready, why don't we get going?" He peered over my shoulder, saw Dad and walked over to shake hands with him.

"Good to see you, Frank. It's been a long time."

Dad smiled. "Sure has, but I won't hold you up. You two get going. I'll hold down the fort."

Once we were in the Jeep, Ross started the engine and headed down the hill. He glanced over at me. "I like your hair down like that."

"Thanks," I said, feeling a blush climb up my neck. "Where are we going anyway?"

He turned onto the Seward Highway and in the direction of Turnagain Arm. "How does the Double Musky sound for dinner? I wanted to leave early because they don't take reservations."

"Mmmhmm. Sounds good. Haven't been there since ski season."

"They're always busy, even this time of year. If we can't get in, we can eat at the Alyeska Resort, but this early I don't think we'll have a problem."

We drove the snakelike curves of the Seward Highway in silence. A bore tide rushed across the water on one side of the road and steep rock walls edged the Chugach State park on the other. Far ahead, the blue ice of a glacier spilled down the Kenai mountains.

Halfway to our destination, I turned to Ross. "FYI, I finally checked our lease on Merrill Field. Dad renewed it shortly before he retired. It's good for another twenty-four years. It remains in effect for a new owner if we sell our building."

"That would make your site more attractive than mine. And, yours is larger." Ross reached the turnoff for Girdwood, turned on Alyeska Highway and headed for the restaurant.

Although the Musky had grown considerably over the years with additions added, the log building still retained its original rustic identity. Once inside, we were happy to see only a short line of prospective diners waiting to be seated.

"We're in luck," Ross said. "Shouldn't be a problem to get in."

It took only five minutes to reach the front of the line. A bearded man holding menus greeted us and showed us to a table.

"Can I bring you anything to drink?" he asked.

"Water for me, thanks," Ross said. "I'm the designated driver. What would you like, Beri?"

"A glass of Chardonnay, please."

Our table was set slightly apart from the others, making it easy to talk. After we placed our orders, I folded my hands on the table and gazed into his eyes. "Now, are you ready to tell me who I need to see so I can get the flight plan tape?"

"Can you free up your schedule Monday afternoon between four and five?"

"I think so. Why?"

"We have an appointment to listen to the tapes."

"You *are* efficient," I said. "Thanks."

"Feel free to express your appreciation in a more tangible way." He covered my hands with his and wiggled his eyebrows.

"C'mon, Ross. We're all grown up now."

His smile broadened. "My point, exactly."

Chapter Eighteen

Claire, my hairdresser, assessed my reflection in the mirror as she effortlessly smoothed my wayward locks into soft curls framing my face.

"Are you sure you don't want an up-do for the gala?" she asked.

"Yes, I'm sure. I want to appear respectable, but I don't want to go overboard. This is a business event only."

"Uh huh. What are you wearing?"

"Haven't decided yet. I have two cocktail dresses—one black and one forest green. I'll choose one of them."

"Which one has the lower neckline?"

"The green one."

"Wear that!"

I laughed. "If you say so. You're incorrigible, you know."

"Do you mind if I give you some advice, Beri?"

"Would it stop you if I did?" I winked at her in the mirror.

"Probably not." She stepped away and reviewed her handiwork. "You're really attractive. You wouldn't have to change much to be truly beautiful."

"Yeah, right." I held up the hand mirror to check the back of my head to assure Claire I was pleased with her efforts. "A daily comb-out from you would go a long way to boost my glamour quotient."

"No. What you need is a touch of surgery to narrow that schnoz of yours. It's just a little too wide."

"That may be, but I'm pretty attached to my nose the way it is." I smiled. "I think I inherited most of my face from my mom, but I definitely did get my dad's nose."

"Your mom must have been gorgeous."

"I guess so. I haven't seen her since I was five. Dad says Alaska was too remote for her, and I don't think she liked motherhood much. She took off. Dad stayed the course and raised me, so I don't mind keeping his nose." I winked at her again. "But thanks for saying I could be beautiful."

Alex, dark and striking in his tux, sat next to me at the mayor's table near the front of the ballroom. I'd met the mayor's wife when our sons played on the same soccer team. We chatted for a few minutes after our dessert plates were cleared.

Alex leaned close and whispered, "I want to tear you away for a dance before they start the program."

I felt a slow tingle go up my spine after he led me to the dance floor and pulled me close. Was it attraction or fear?

He held his head to the side. "I like dancing with the best-looking woman in the room."

I glanced up at him and blushed despite my best efforts not to. There was something about his face—lean, handsome, fierce.

The music stopped and the mayor stepped up to the microphone. "Ladies and gentlemen. If you will please take your seats, we will begin our program."

Alex steered me to our chairs as the mayor continued.

"As you know, our function tonight is a fundraiser in support of Kids Are Our Future, an organization that promotes programs to help insure all children get a good start in life, especially those with physical, mental or economic challenges. I hope each and every one of you will generously participate in our silent auction. A large variety of wonderful items donated by local businesses are displayed on tables in the foyer. A list of these can be found in tonight's program.

"At this time, I want to give special recognition to our guest of honor, Alex Veronin, president of Cartos, a San Francisco photogrammetry and mapping company, for his generous donation of time and money to our cause. We are pleased to accept his check for $200,000, bringing us very near to meeting our financial goal for the year. Alex, will you come forward please?"

As Alex approached, the mayor reached out, shook his hand and presented him with an ornate plaque. "Please accept this as a small token of our city's appreciation."

After the applause subsided, Alex spoke into the microphone. "Thank you, Mr. Mayor. It has been my pleasure to support such a wonderful organization."

Alex returned to his seat and placed the plaque on the table in front of him. "Will look good on the wall of our corporate office," he said to me.

The mayor continued, "We will now proceed with tonight's entertainment, Mr. Kenny G and his wonderful saxophone."

After the last strains of "Forever in Love" faded and the applause ended, Alex touched my hand. "Are you ready to go? Let's stop at the bar and have a drink. There's something I want to talk to you about."

I picked up my clutch. "Ready when you are."

We said our good-byes and walked down the staircase to the hotel's cocktail lounge, found a table and ordered drinks.

"Sorry if I rushed you out a little early," Alex said.

"Not a problem, I was ready. Congratulations for the award by the way."

"It's nothing. They only honor me because I gave them money."

"A worthy cause, none-the-less."

"Yes, can't go wrong helping children."

I took a sip of my stinger. "You wanted to talk to me about business. Do you have another project for us?"

"No, nothing like that. What I want is to buy your company."

"Buy it?" I tried hard not to drop my drink.

"Yes, it's time Cartos acquired a foothold of our own in the Alaskan market. We will make you a very generous offer."

"But it's a family business. My dad built it. I can't sell it."

"Why not? I happen to know your finances are shaky at best. We've been one of your best customers. Without us, I don't think you'd make it."

"True, you've been a great help and I hope we can continue doing business with you, but I don't want to sell to anybody."

His jaw hardened and he stared through me. "Our previous arrangement has reached an end, Beri. You must now consider us your competitor."

"But…"

Alex held up his hand. "No argument. Our decision has been made. We are moving into the Alaskan market ourselves."

"I'm sorry to hear that." I stood up. "I'd like to go home now, please."

Chapter Nineteen

The next morning, I found Dean in the Roto-Tech hangar huddled with two helicopter mechanics. He talked, gesturing rapidly with his hands and appeared unusually animated.

The conversation tapered off when I approached. "What's happening, guys?"

"Not much. We were discussing the preliminary FAA report on the crash. I'll fill you in later." Dean took my arm. "We need to go to the office so you can sign some papers."

After we'd walked outside the hearing of the mechanics, Dean spoke softly to me. "You asked me to take charge of retrieving the plane. Just to let you know, Angie's upset. She thinks we should leave it where it is and save the money."

"Sounds like Angie. I don't think she understands we're obligated to remove the wreckage unless it's too dangerous to recover. Besides, we need to examine it. We may be able to salvage enough parts to cover some of the expense. I'll talk to her."

"So we're good to go?"

"Yes. We don't have a choice. What do you estimate it will cost?"

"The FAA retrieved part of the plane already to inspect the fuel system. The crew here can bring the rest by helicopter. They deliver supplies to a village near the accident site. Since they'll be in the area they can bring the plane as far as Lake Iliamna cheap. From there, we can catch a charter cargo plane on an empty return flight."

I nodded. "Good job figuring that out."

We arrived at my desk. Dean took a clipboard with paperwork from the secretary and handed it to me.

"Thanks. I need to get moving. I have a meeting at the FAA office this afternoon." I placed the signed paperwork on the desk and turned to leave.

Dean frowned. "About that meeting. Be careful."

"Aren't I always?"

"You are, but rumor has it they're saying you failed to check the sumps for condensation. They're going for a finding of pilot error."

"*What?* Of course I checked. I always do."

The FAA receptionist informed me the team would be with me in a few minutes. I took a seat and nervously adjusted my skirt. Fortunately, my gray suit still fit. Brightened with a pomegranate silk shirt and matching pumps, I was reasonably presentable.

"Right this way. They're ready for you now," the receptionist said.

She led me to a small conference room starkly furnished with a large government-issued table, four chairs and not much else. Two men in business suits and one woman sat around the table. The woman, thin to the point of bony, wore a severe black dress. With her hair styled in a short ultra-sleek bob, she appeared more East-Coast professional than local bureaucrat. Maybe she aspired to a rapid climb up the career ladder. She stood, pulled out the empty chair at the end of the table and motioned for me to sit.

"Thank you for coming, Ms. Quinn. As you know, we've convened this meeting as part of our investigation of your plane crash on August 12, of this year." She switched on a device at her side. "We will be recording this session. My name is Marianne Hermann. I'm the chief investigator. This is Evan Tutwilder, and I think you've met Larry Lindsey previously."

"Yes. Thank you," I acknowledged.

"For the record, Ms. Quinn, we'd like you to relate for us the events leading to the crash. Start from the beginning, please."

"All right," I said. "I began the flight by following my pre-flight checklist step by step. As part of this process, I checked both sumps for fuel condensation, draining each of them until the color ran clear blue. It wasn't hazy. Next, I started the engine, checked the gauges, contacted the tower and took off on runway 33 to the north, with a Ship Creek departure."

"When did you first experience signs of trouble?" the chairwoman asked.

"Just over an hour into the flight. The engine sputtered, and the plane began vibrating."

She kept her gaze steady. "How did you respond?"

"I adjusted my fuel mixture, switched tanks, turned on my boost pump and the carburetor heat. Nothing helped. I radioed I had an emergency."

"Then what?"

"I searched for a safe place to land in case we needed it. That's when the engine stopped completely."

"What made you choose that particular landing spot?" Larry Lindsey asked.

I glanced his way. "I chose a flat grassy area along the river. It appeared smooth enough. I ruled out the sandbars because they were too small."

"So what happened next?" the chairwoman asked.

"I hit a log hidden in the grass, and the plane cartwheeled."

"You're telling us you had no idea there was a log there?" Lindsey asked.

"No, I didn't. It was completely hidden by the tall grass."

"Was there fire?"

"I half-expected there might be, but no, there wasn't any."

The chairwoman stood. "Gentlemen, do you have any further questions?"

No one spoke.

"Hearing none, I'll thank you Ms. Quinn. We have what we need," she said, bringing the session to an end.

I remained seated. "Before we leave, may I ask what your investigation of the wreckage showed?"

"You'll receive a copy of our report when it is completed, but I can tell you that there were findings inconsistent with your version of events," Ms. Hermann said.

"Really?" I asked. "Can you be more specific?"

"We found clear evidence of fuel contamination. Water in the fuel explains the engine failure. If you checked the sumps as you stated, you would have prevented that. At this point, it appears our report will indicate pilot negligence due to failure to properly follow pre-flight requirements."

"But I did check."

"So you say, but I'm afraid the findings speak for themselves. You should be aware that if the final report is what we expect, you could be facing possible license suspension and even criminal charges."

"Criminal charges?" My stomach spun into my throat. This wasn't possible. "I'd like to have the fuel tested by an independent lab before the final report is released. I'll also want a copy of your appeal process regulations."

"That's certainly your prerogative, especially since an aggravated assault charge is a distinct possibility. After all, your passenger suffered broken bones which is grounds for felony charges if negligence is proven. I haven't seen the results of your drug and alcohol tests yet, but if it's positive, that would be an additional factor." The chairwoman swept a small tendril of hair that had escaped captivity back into place. "Of course, whether to bring charges will be up to the prosecutors. I'm just giving you a head's up. You may want to find yourself an attorney, Ms. Quinn." With that warning, Marianne Hermann adjourned the meeting.

I tried hard to hold it together as I departed the room. *Criminal charges? License suspension?* First Ken's disappearance, then Buzz's murder, and now this? I dared not think what could be next.

Chapter Twenty

"**D**ad, I've got problems," I said. I had to tell someone, and I didn't feel comfortable discussing the situation with Dean or Angie. I hadn't slept all night.

Dad stood in the garage working on a chest he was making to store Jack's off-season sports gear. I walked over and perched on a spindly stool next to his work bench.

"Problems? What kind?"

I met with the FAA investigative team yesterday, and it didn't go well."

"How so?" Dad swiveled to face me, a puzzled expression on his face. "It was just a formality, wasn't it?"

"No, it wasn't. That's what I expected, but what happened felt hostile."

"Come on. What could they possibly get uptight about? It was an accident. You didn't screw anything up."

"I know, but that isn't the way they see it. They're claiming I didn't check for moisture in the fuel lines during my pre-check."

"Ridiculous! You? Sounds like they're pumped up on their own power and want to intimidate you."

"This all makes me so angry." I slammed my hand against the work bench.

"Ouch!" I brushed small splinters of wood from my palm. "I don't get it. I hate to sound paranoid, but it feels like they're skewing the investigation against me."

"Sounds like they're testing you, hoping they can trick you into making an admission of wrongdoing. Hire a lawyer. You need to protect yourself." He put his arm over my shoulder and drew me close. "Come on, let's go start breakfast. Jack will be waking up soon."

Halfway through sourdough pancakes, the phone rang.

"I'll get it." Jack jumped up and ran to the phone. "Hi, Dad." Jack listened without talking for several minutes. "That sounds great! Okay, here's Mom."

I took the receiver and walked out of the room.

"How're you doing, Beri?" my ex said. "Jack sounds good."

"We're fine, thanks."

"Did Jack tell you we want to take him to Europe with us?"

"*What?* No, he didn't tell me." Jack and I would have to have a heart-to-heart about this.

"Well, he sounded excited about it. Felicity and I are planning to spend two months driving through Europe and we want to take him with us. It'll be a great opportunity for him."

"When are you planning this?"

"We think we can pull it together to leave next month. We want to do it while the weather's still nice. It's the last year we can do it before Janna starts kindergarten next year."

"What about Jack? He can't miss that much school."

"No problem. We've already talked about that. Felicity says she can home school him while we travel, and he can finish the school year here."

"Sure, he can. Are you crazy, Dennis? He can't leave all his friends and start over mid-year in a new school."

"I think you're over-reacting. Why don't you talk to Jack and think about it before you decide?"

"I'll do that, thank you very much." I returned to the kitchen and hung up the phone with a thud.

Dad turned his head and gave me a look. "What was that all about? That phone's not going to last long if you treat it that way."

"I just wish Dennis would use his brain for a change," I said. "He wants Jack to fly down next week to go on vacation with his family. They're planning to drive through as much of Europe as they can manage in two months' time."

"Yeah, it sounds awesome," Jack said.

"Why all of a sudden and why now?" Dad asked.

"He realized his step-daughter would start school next year and they didn't want her to miss any. Of course, it doesn't bother him that Jack would miss school now."

"Mom," Jack said. "Dad said I could go to school in Arizona and live with him. School doesn't start as early there, and he can get a tutor to help me catch up."

Dad placed the dishes in the sink and sprayed off the crumbs and syrup before racking them in the dishwasher. "Jack, like we said before, there's no way you can miss the state tournament. You know your team's in the finals."

"Like I already told you, they don't need me," Jack said. "I mostly sit on the bench anyway."

"That's an important job," I said. "What if someone gets sick?"

"Mom, I want to see my dad. I haven't seen him all year."

"That's because he cancelled your scheduled visit when school let out, and we've already made plans for you to spend Christmas vacation with him." I felt torn because the trip would be an educational opportunity, but no way could Jack miss that much school. There'd be other chances for him to travel.

"I don't care about a stupid baseball tournament. I want to go to school in Arizona. I want to live with my dad!" Jack stormed up the stairs to his room, Tiger following close behind.

Dad finished loading the dishwasher. "You go on. You don't want to be late for work. I'll take care of things here."

"I feel bad," I said. "I don't want to keep him from his father, and Europe would be exciting. But what Jack doesn't realize is that Dennis's wife seems to resent having him around. Can you imagine two months in a car with her? Followed by living with her during the rest of the school year? And her having to homeschool him?"

Dad shook his head. "No, Dennis never has been very practical."

"That's an understatement."

"Maybe Felicity has mellowed some by now."

I picked up my jacket and purse, and started toward the door to the garage. "I think I'll let Jack cool down before we talk more about it. Give me a call if he gives me any problems."

"Will do, cupcake."

The hangar door was closed when I parked outside and went into the office.

"Good morning, Angie, what's the schedule today?" I asked, smiling at her as I made my way to my desk.

"Really light for you. Richard's got a student this morning and two more this afternoon." She stared up at me. "Hey, are you okay? You look like you had a rough night."

"Rough morning's more like it. You know, family stuff. Nothing to worry about."

"Jack and your Dad at each other again?"

"No, that's not it this time. Dennis called, and our conversation was contentious, that's all. I'd rather not talk about it. I want to put it out of my mind for now."

"Fine by me. How did the FAA meeting go yesterday?"

"Another topic I want to avoid. How are your kids doing?"

Angie laughed. "They're evil, but I love 'em. The Boys and Girls Club will rejoice when they're back in school."

I sat at my desk and turned on the computer to check weather patterns in areas I had photography jobs pending. "Have you seen Dean?"

"Yes. I was supposed to tell you to call him on his cell. Says he's found something interesting, whatever that means."

I hoped whatever he found was good news. I didn't know how much more bad news I could take.

Roto-Tech's hangar wasn't empty this time. I spotted the desolate remains of my plane heaped against one wall. Parked next to it was a Huey 205, its cowling still warm. What a sad ending for what had been my favorite bird. It was my stalwart companion since I started the flight school and had served me well.

Dean and another mechanic were examining tubing dangling from the carburetor. They were so absorbed in their scrutiny they hadn't noticed me come in.

"What's so interesting?" I asked. "You're examining that thing so closely, you might as well put it under a microscope."

"Wouldn't be a bad idea," Roto-Tech's mechanic said.

"It don't look good, Beri," Dean said.

"Why? What did you find?" I asked.

"You tell her, Dean. I've got to go do the work I get paid for. Good luck, you two."

Dean put the remnant of the plane down on a work bench and turned to me. "We found part of a zip-lock bag in the fuel line."

"What?"

"My guess is someone dropped a sandwich baggie filled with water into your fuel tank and most of the plastic dissolved in the gasoline."

"But wouldn't I have noticed that when I did my pre-check? The water would still have shown up when I drained the sump."

"Maybe not," Dean shrugged. "It depends on how long the bag was in there. Maybe it hadn't dissolved yet. Perhaps that was the whole idea."

"It would explain why the FAA found water. But wouldn't the plastic you found have blocked the fuel line anyway?"

"It probably did. We need to notify the FAA investigators."

"I'll give them a call right now." I can't believe they would ignore this kind of evidence. *Or could they?*

Chapter Twenty-one

The last of the Rainy Pass photos arrived. Angie jumped up and brought the package in to me. "Finally," she said. "Finally, we can bill Paige."

"Yes, I'll give her a call and let her know our last batch of pictures came. You can have the invoice ready when she comes in."

"That's a relief," Angie said. "You wouldn't believe how many phone calls I've been getting every day demanding we pay bills. Our outflow has exceeded our inflow since that last payment from the Cartos job. I hope we're going to do more work for them soon."

"As things stand now, that's not going to happen, but I plan to work on it. They could definitely help our bottom line." I slipped a disc into my computer. "Meanwhile, I'll scan these photos since the weather isn't cooperating with any of my other projects."

Paige arrived a short time later. "Glad the pictures actually came. I was about to give up on them."

I ran my hand down the stack of discs. "Well, they're here. Now we can get down to work. It'll take a while to go through them all."

"If I can take some home, I have a geologist friend who could help us screen them."

"Good idea," I said. "I have two copies. We can keep a complete set here and divvy up the other."

Angie walked into my office and handed Paige the invoice. "Here you go.

Now that you have all the photos, I'm hoping you can settle this today."

"Oh," Paige said. "I guess I thought it would be due when we found Ken, but I'll start working on getting the money." She glanced at me.

"I'm glad to hear it," Angie said, "because the invoices for the film and gas are due now."

It bothered me that Angie was so aggressive about collecting from Paige. She carries things too far sometimes, but she's fiercely loyal and is a critical member of our team. I think the time has come to send her for some customer relations training. Our clients deserve more respect. She's so good at everything else, I'd overlooked her attitude problem too long.

"Richard will need the remaining 180 for the two students he has this afternoon," I said, after scanning the flight schedule. "We're running out of airplanes."

"Isn't that the truth?" Angie said. "We're down to the 170, one Cub and 180 and the twin. And it appears the insurance company plans to take their time paying for replacements. They say they're waiting to see if Ken is found before closing that claim. We'll see how long they'll take on our latest loss."

"I'll take the twin. The weather's clearing, so I'll have a chance to photograph the area around Ken's prospecting sites."

"More pictures? I thought you were finished." Angie shook her head mother-hen style.

"Relax. It'll be just a few this time."

Both the flight to Ken's site and the return trip were uneventful. No plane problems, thank God. I unloaded my equipment, stashed it in the empty office and collapsed into my chair. It was dinner time, but I didn't feel emotionally ready to resume my debate with Jack. I clicked on my computer and turned to the internet. Jack's birthday would be here soon, and I'd often thought he would enjoy a birding trip to Saint Paul Island, a birder's paradise. It would be fun to take a short vacation together, but it'd be tight to squeeze it in before school started. I jotted down lodging information, closed the office and started home.

Jack had finished eating by the time I got there. I sat next to him on the sofa and handed him the print-out. "Happy Birthday!"

"What's this?"

"I thought a birding trip would be fun for both of us. Saint Paul Island has over 200 species of birds, some only found in Alaska. It'll be a great experience."

Jack glanced at me, but seemed subdued. The usual excitement I expected to see from him wasn't there. "Thanks," he said, stood and went toward the stairs.

"I think I'll go to bed now."

"Not exactly overwhelmed by enthusiasm," Dad said.

"No, but he'll love it when we get there." Undeterred, I got online and scheduled the trip. With our tight timeline, I didn't want to be left with no vacancies. It would be hard to take time away from the search for Ken, but I couldn't neglect Jack.

The next morning at breakfast, Jack fiddled with his scrambled eggs before finally giving up and putting his fork down.

"What's wrong, Jack? Aren't you hungry?"

He grimaced. "Mom, I don't want to go."

"Don't want to go? But you love birds. Don't you want to add a red-legged kittiwake or a Lapland longspur to your life list?"

"Sure, but I feel like you're bribing me."

"Bribing you? How?"

"Not to go with Dad." He put his fork down and stood up. "I don't think you're being fair. You never wanted to take me there before."

"Maybe not, but you've never been turning eleven years old before. It's your birthday present."

"Yeah, right," Jack turned his back to me and started upstairs.

"Wait. I wasn't thinking of it that way. We'd already decided you couldn't go to Europe with your dad."

"You mean you decided," Jack said, rubbing tears from his eyes. "I still want to go with Dad."

I felt like crying myself.

Chapter Twenty-two

I stopped at Gracie Higgin's law office on my way to work. It was a longshot that I'd catch her. But if she wasn't available, I'd make an appointment. The small office was located in a business complex, and I took the mostly empty parking spaces outside as a good sign.

The receptionist gave me a big smile. "How can I help you?"

"My name is Beri Quinn. I'd like to see Gracie for a few minutes, if she can squeeze me in."

"Just a moment. I'll check with her." She returned a moment later. "We're in luck. You caught her at a good time."

She led me down a short hallway to Gracie's office, a comfortable room decorated with photographs of historic Alaskan gold mines.

"This is a nice surprise, Beri. How are you?" Gracie asked.

"I'm fine, but I'm afraid this isn't a social visit." I sat in one of the rustic chairs in front of her desk. "I have a few legal questions for you."

Gracie moved around her desk and sat in the chair next to me. "Tell me about it."

"First, I need legal representation for an FAA inquiry into a recent incident. Can you recommend anyone who specializes in that kind of thing?"

"Sure." She scribbled a couple of names on a slip of paper. "Either of these guys would be good."

"Thanks, Gracie." I paused, then took a deep breath. "My next problem is about my son, Jack."

"Oh, what's the problem?"

"I'm worried about losing custody. Dennis wants him to take two months off school to travel across Europe with his new family. In fact, Dennis suggested he live with him afterward and attend school in Arizona. Jack is excited about the whole idea."

"You're not, I take it."

"No," I said, not meeting her eyes. "I'd like him to travel someday, but I don't want him to miss two months of school. I really don't want Jack to live with Dennis, either."

"How old is Jack now? Twelve?"

"He'll be eleven in a few weeks."

"Is Dennis a good father?"

I twisted in my chair. "He has a bad habit of not following through with his promises."

"Does he love Jack?"

"He does, yes. That's genuine."

"Has he kept up with child support?"

"Yes."

"The reason I ask all this is that Jack is approaching the age when the court is likely to allow the child to choose which parent to live with when there's a dispute."

"You're kidding?" My voice rose louder than I'd intended.

"No. Courts will often take that approach especially by age fourteen, but at eleven or twelve it's also a distinct possibility. I assume there's been regular visitation?"

"Yes, on and off."

"Beri, I know this isn't what you want to hear, but I can tell you that it's extremely common for children of divorced parents to romanticize the non-custodial parent and want to go live with them. Unless you're worried about Jack's safety, it may be the wisest course to let him go. Odds are good that he'll be anxious to come home after they return from Europe. If you clamp down too hard he may rebel even more."

"So you think I should let him go?" I asked in disbelief.

"What I think is that you should give this a lot of thought before you refuse to let him go."

The day went quickly with two students in the morning and a small flying job in the Matanuska Valley in the early afternoon. I was glad to stay busy to avoid obsessing about what to do about Jack.

At four, I met Ross at his office. He'd suggested we drive together to meet his friend who worked at the Flight Standards District Office, or FSDO, a branch of the FAA commonly referred to as FIZZDO. Ross thought he might be able to help me get a copy of Ken's flight plan tape.

Ross met me as I got out of my car and gave me a quick hug.

"Ready?" he asked. "Let's hop in the Jeep. The office closes at four. My friend, Don, doesn't expect anyone will still be around by the time we get there."

"Sounds very covert. Are flight plan recordings really that confidential?"

"Guess so. You can ask him."

The FSDO building was located to the southwest, near Lake Hood and Lake Spenard, the major floatplane base in the state. The two lakes, connected by channels, are ringed wingtip to wingtip by pontoon planes. These were the most coveted tie-down spaces in Anchorage. The waiting time for a permanent slot on water's edge is at least ten years, and that's with a lot of luck.

Ross took International Airport Road and turned into the less scenic industrial freight area. As predicted, the parking lot in front of the building was almost empty. A tall man in his thirties let us in and stooped to lock the door behind us.

He turned to me. "You must be Beri. I'm Don. Nice meeting you." He shook my hand, turned and preceded us down the hall. "We need to go this way."

We entered a room barely larger than a closet. The walls were lined with shelves of books and tapes. A small table in the center of the room held electronic equipment and headphones. A few folding chairs were also crammed in the room.

"Here we are," he said, turning to face me. "Have a seat. Now, what exactly is it you want to hear?"

"I'm anxious to listen to the flight plan one of my students filed last July seventeenth. His tail number was November 2789 Echo. I'm hoping you have it on file."

"Sorry to disappoint, but probably not. We usually keep tapes for only fifteen days."

"Usually, you said. Are there any circumstances when you keep them longer?"

Don turned toward one of the shelves full of tapes. "Yes, we can keep them up to five years if an accident is involved. The National Transportation and Safety Board may want to review them, and they may be subpoenaed in the case of a lawsuit."

"Great," I said. "That could apply here. The plane went missing and was assumed to have crashed. Could you check for the date?"

"He departed Merrill?"

After I nodded, he scanned the shelves and pulled out a tape.

"This would be the one if we have it. I'll set it up for you." He handed me a set of headphones. "We'll need to scroll through a bit. What time did he file, or do you know?"

"My guess would be sometime mid-morning."

After consulting a log of entries, he pushed a few buttons and announced he thought he'd found what I wanted. "Let's listen."

Pilot: *"November 2789 Echo. Will be departing Merrill Field at thirty minutes past the hour. Route of flight will be Anchorage up the Yentna River to Skwentna, Rainy Pass to Parallel Lake direct to McGrath. Cruising altitude VFR. Time in route two and half hours, four hours fuel, one soul on board. I'll open the flight plan with flight service after airborne. Have emergency beacon and gear. Pilot's name is Ken Abbott."*

Tower: *"Do you have current weather and notice to airmen report?"*

Pilot: *"I checked a few hours ago and it looked good to me."*

Don stopped the tape and turned to me. "What do you think?"

"It's off somehow. For one thing, Ken wouldn't rely on a weather report that wasn't up to the minute. He knows how fast conditions change."

Something else bothered me, but I couldn't quite place it. It just didn't sound right.

Don scanned further down the log. "I don't see the plan he posted in flight." He shrugged and ran his finger further down the log, then returned to the top. "Guess that's it."

He started to remove the tape, but stopped. "Oh, wait a minute. Maybe I do see another one, but it's earlier than the one we just heard."

"Let's hear it too," I said, feeling a shiver of excitement.

Don played the entry. This time, Ken filed a similar report to Alice Creek.

"Now that makes more sense. That's where he originally said he was going," I said. "And now I know what was bothering me before."

"What?" Ross asked.

"His Boston accent. It was missing in the first recording. Someone else filed that plan to McGrath."

"Why would they do that?" Ross asked.

"I don't know, but I intend to find out. It wasn't Ken, I'm sure of it."

Chapter Twenty-three

I'd barely returned to the office when Alex Veronin strode in. I stood to meet him.

"Hello, Alex. I didn't know you were in Alaska."

"I just arrived. Had some business dealings to take care of and thought I'd stop by because I wanted to talk to you." He glanced over at Angie. "Privately."

"I'm getting ready to leave," Angie said.

"What I had in mind was to talk over drinks," Alex said. "My hotel's close. Let's go to the bar there." He took my arm and guided me a few steps toward the door. "We can go together in my car."

"The bar is fine, but I'll drive myself. I'm scheduled to meet someone later this evening and won't be able to stay long."

"Have it your way, Beri. I'll meet you at the Sheraton in ten minutes." He pushed open the door and left.

Angie turned to look at me. "He comes on a bit strong, don'tcha think?"

I laughed. "He can be brusque, but if I can win back his business, I'll humor him."

"Brusque and sexy, too. Good luck," Angie whispered as I left.

The hotel lobby was empty except for two business types checking in at the front desk. I walked past the massive curved staircase built of Alaskan jade and into the bar. Alex's drink was already on the table.

"I started without you." He motioned to the waitress. "What will you have?"

I sat across from him. "A glass of white wine, please."

"That's not a drink. Sure you don't want something stronger?"

"I have another meeting, remember? Wine is fine."

"All right." He finished his drink in one great swallow. "Bring me another as well," he said to the waitress.

"So what's up? Any new business we can do for you?" I asked.

"No. Like I told you before, we're done with that." He stared at me across the table. "I'm here to talk some sense into you. I've reviewed your financials. You're about to go under, and I'm prepared to make you an offer you can't refuse."

"Hold on…"

"No. You're beyond having a choice. You need to sell. It's your one best chance."

"Of course, I have a choice. As I've tried to explain…"

"I'm sorry," Alex interrupted, "But you need to face reality here. You can't survive without my business, and I'm not sending you any more of it. Besides, I understand you have big problems with the FAA and one of your employees was murdered. I'm offering you a way out of your troubles. I'm offering you six million dollars. Cash."

I gulped. Much as I loved my business, it was worth much less. "That's a lot of money," I said.

"I'm in town for only one week. I want to get this done before I leave."

"I wasn't expecting that kind of offer," I said. "Let me think about it."

"Think if you like, but think fast. People who refuse offers like this don't end up well."

"Are you threatening me, Alex?" I stood up, leaving my drink untouched.

"No, just offering practical advice. You have a family to consider."

I stalked out of the bar, barely keeping my composure.

I skipped my imaginary meeting and went straight home. I didn't want to sell, but this was scary. I needed to think, and I needed to talk to Dad. On the way, I pulled off at Potter's Marsh and got out to walk and think. Not many people were on the boardwalk this evening. I gazed down through the grasses and plant life rising above the shallow waters of the marsh. I spotted a spawning salmon, its normally silver skin blushed a rosy hue in the last hours of its life. Somehow, even though marred by the noise from neighboring Seward Highway, I always found the marsh a place of serenity, a place to sort my confused thoughts.

I knew the decision I should make. Jack needed to go with his father so why was I so conflicted? While I pondered, a bald eagle dove at the grass intent on his prey and rose with something small wriggling in his talons. A field mouse or shrew?

I guess that was what was troubling me really. Jack was so defenseless if Dennis disappointed him yet again, and considering his track record, the odds were good he would.

I strolled the length of the walkway, wishing I'd brought my binoculars. The marsh teemed with water fowl, but most birds were wise enough to keep some distance from the viewing area. A couple of mallards and a golden-eye paddled close by, one of them plunging its head below the surface, leaving its tail feathers pointing comically at the sky.

As I returned to the car, I noticed a flurry of interest by tourists at the other end of the parking lot. I drove slowly in that direction and spotted a moose and her calf munching willows, unperturbed by the spectators thirty yards away. The mother moose never took her eyes off the humans lest they approach too close to her offspring. The sight reminded me that I should get home to my family.

As I walked in the door, Jack rushed up. "Gramps said the Jeters called. They're over their flu bug, and it's okay for him to visit them in Nome now. He left about an hour ago."

"He's already gone? He didn't call me."

"Yeah. Said you'd be home any time now, and he'd be back in about three days."

"Well then, it looks like it's just you and me, Bub. Let's get started on some dinner."

I spent a restless night. When I finally drifted off to sleep I woke again an hour later, my mind still trying to process the day's events. Veronin's threat seemed unreal, but I couldn't afford to take any chances. Not able to talk to Dad about the situation, I needed to talk to someone.

There was only one person I could think of who would be up this early. I dialed Ross's cell number and hoped I didn't wake him.

"Hello. Is that you, Beri?"

"Yes. Sorry to call at this hour, but I need some advice badly right now."

"Of course. I'll do my best."

"Remember our talking about someone wanting to force you out of business?" I paused. "Well, it's happening to me, too. Big time."

"Tell me."

I gave him a rundown of my conversation with Alex Veronin. "I felt he was threatening me. And, Ross, I'm beginning to wonder if he hasn't played a role in some of the other problems I've been having."

"And here I've been thinking he was sweet on you. Sounds like you should go to the cops. Tell them about the threat."

"I will, but I doubt they can do anything." My voice cracked. "And I'm afraid he might retaliate by doing something to Jack."

"Jack? Why?"

"He mentioned I needed to protect my family. I'm not sure what he meant."

"It could have been an empty threat?"

"I keep asking myself what to do? Selling the business would solve almost all my problems. The bills would get paid, the FAA investigation would be much less intimidating. I'd have a lot of money, and we'd be safe. How can I refuse?"

"When you put it that way…"

"On the other hand, it goes against everything I believe in to let myself be bullied into giving up the business I love, especially when I suspect Alex's motives for buying it. But how can I keep Jack safe while I fight to keep it?"

"You need to warn Frank. He'll keep him safe."

"Dad's up north and won't return for several days."

"Bring Jack over to my office for safe keeping this morning. I'll put him to work washing airplanes. Tell him he can earn some spending money."

"That would be great. Thanks." I clicked off the phone and stood thinking. The answer was obvious even as I struggled to accept it. It was the last thing I thought I would ever do, but I picked up the phone and called Dennis.

A tired Jack greeted me when I stopped at Ross's hangar to pick him up.

"Mom, come see! I cleaned two whole airplanes and earned twenty dollars." He grinned happily. "Ross says I do good work."

"He does, too. I'll call him again when I need my planes washed." Ross gave me a questioning look. "Everything good?"

"Yes, I think so." I turned to Jack. "Hop in the car, mister. We'll go home in a few minutes."

I walked a few feet away and leaned toward Ross. "Let's step over here for a minute."

"Sure thing," he said and followed me.

"Dennis agreed to move up Jack's trip to Arizona. I'm taking him to the airport tonight, and they'll leave next week for Europe. At least this way I know he'll be safe."

Ross squeezed my shoulder. "Did you call the cops?"

"Yes. They took my statement, but I think the only reason they were interested was because of the murder."

"Stay vigilant, Beri, and call me if there's anything I can do to help."

"Thanks. I appreciate it."

As I drove Jack to the house, I turned to him. "I talked to your dad, and he said he bought a ticket for you to leave later tonight. We'll need to get home and get you packed."

Jack's eyes lit up. "Really? I'm going?"

"Yes. They plan to leave for Germany by the end of the week."

"Thanks, Mom. I know you didn't want me to go."

"It's not that I didn't want you to go. I do want you to visit Europe, Jack. It's a great opportunity." I smiled at him. "I have to admit though, I'll miss you. A lot."

Jack faced me. "I love you, Mom. I won't be gone forever, you know."

I ruffled his hair. "I know."

Chapter Twenty-four

The house felt much too quiet with Dad and Jack both gone. I clicked the television on and stretched out on the sofa. Tiger lay on the floor beside me. I was lonely, missing Jack and Dad, too. What had I done sending Jack off to be with Dennis? I couldn't survive if my son didn't come back. But he would. Wouldn't he?

I drifted off to sleep snuggled under a Pendleton throw I scrounged from Dad's recliner and woke at my usual five o'clock. I was grateful my lack of sleep the previous night helped me overcome insomnia.

I dressed, took Tiger for a quick walk, fed him and sat down to a bowl of Cheerios. After rinsing my bowl, I scratched Tiger's ears. "Sorry to leave you boy, but I have work to do."

In the office, I sat at my computer and cancelled the birding trip, hoping I'd get at least a partial refund. I thought about postponing it, but without knowing exactly when Jack would return, it seemed pointless. Maybe next year.

The office phone rang. Angie answered and pushed the hold button. "It's Alex Veronin for you on line one."

"Tell him I'm not here."

Angie raised her eyebrows, but did her duty. "I'm sorry, she must have just left. Can I take a message?"

Angie disconnected. "Okay, Beri. Give. What's up with you and that man?"

"I'm not ready to deal with him right now." I rummaged through my purse. "I need to leave the office before Alex comes by and discovers you were lying for me. Sorry, but I'll have to fill you in later." Frustrated, I dumped the contents on my desk.

"What are you doing?" Angie asked. "I thought you said you were in a hurry."

"I'm trying to find a business card. I know it's in here somewhere." At least, I knew Norm Underwood gave me one with his FBI office number. I wanted to talk to someone who could advise me about what to do about Alex's threats and Norm was the only one I could think of who might help.

I finally found the card, stuffed the remaining contents inside my purse, and dialed while walking to my car. "Norm, this is Beri Quinn. Any chance I could meet with you briefly sometime today?"

"Is this about Ken?" he asked. "I really don't know any more than I told you before."

"No, this is about something else."

"I have a few minutes now before a meeting scheduled in midtown at ten. How about Barnes and Noble on Northern Lights? I can meet you in their coffee shop in fifteen minutes."

"I'll see you then. Thanks, Norm."

I arrived at Barnes and Noble first and found a corner table. Norm walked in, waved hello and tapped the keys of his phone while he waited for his order. Cup in hand, he walked over to the table, and swung one of the chairs around so he could face the room. "Force of habit," he said with a smile. "So you have my attention. What gives?"

"A series of things. You know about Ken already. After that, we had problems with mislabeled aircraft parts. We reported the issue to the FAA, but so far nothing seems to be happening about the problem. Next, the big one. An employee was murdered in a drive-by outside our hangar. No suspects as far as I know. Finally, someone sabotaged my plane, causing me to make a crash landing that injured my passenger. The resulting FAA investigation may jeopardize my license." I took a deep breath. "None of this seems related and maybe it's not, but I have to wonder because now I think I'm being threatened."

Norm sat across from me, his hands steepled together, a slight frown on his face. "Threatened? How?"

I leaned forward. "Are you familiar with a man named Alex Veronin? He's with Cartos, a California mapping company."

"The name is familiar, yes."

"He wants to buy my business. I've resisted selling to him so far, but he's made an offer he thought I couldn't refuse. More money than the company is worth and enough to tempt me, but also enough to make me question why he wants it. I asked for time to think it over, and he pushed to close the deal by the end of this week or else."

"Or else what?"

"That's the thing. I don't know specifically. He implied my family could suffer if I didn't go along with the deal."

"Could be a threat all right." He cleared his throat. "Have you had any dealings with organized crime?"

"*What?* No, of course not. Why?"

"Veronin and his company are known to be connected. Are you sure you've never done business with him?"

"We've done some sub-contract work for Cartos. Aerial photography for mapping projects. All above board."

"Hmm. Any idea why he'd want your company?"

"Not really." I paused. "Well, a competitor mentioned he thought someone was trying to force him out of business recently. He thought it might be someone wanting to take over our leases on Merrill Field."

"He could have something there. Aviation is a prime target for money laundering. It's a business that can move a lot of cash, and the equipment and technology involved can be rapidly depreciated. Mapping offers opportunities for "trade" laundering—inflating pricing on the books. Veronin could be planning to establish a base of operations in Alaska."

"But why me? My business is a small operation."

"That probably *is* the reason. He needs a legitimate location doing work he's already associated with in California and possibly other states. Your small size reduces his total investment. He might also like your particular location for his purposes."

"Our location is a central one. And I checked, the lease would transfer with the building if it's sold."

"I'm not familiar with the legalities of the Municipality's leases, but it doesn't sound like he'd have any problem taking it over if he buys you out. It's also possible he has connections inside the system that could help him grease the wheels."

"What would you suggest I do?"

He was quiet for a moment. Then shrugged. "Unfortunately, there's not much you can do. Take all the safety precautions you can. Report any developments to me and to the police, especially if he tries to do any harm. Unless we have evidence he's broken the law, he's in the clear."

"Not reassuring."

"No, I'm afraid not. I wish I had better news. Have you discussed the situation with your family?"

"Not yet. My dad's out of town for a couple of days. I sent my son to be with his father out of state for the short term."

"Sounds like a good move. You might consider staying with someone or having someone stay with you—at least until your dad returns."

"Thanks, but I can take care of myself. I have a dog, and if I need it, a gun."

"I hope it doesn't come to that."

"Yeah. Me, too, Norm."

Chapter Twenty-five

"You'll be rich. Not that I want to lose my job, but you'd be crazy not to sell," Angie said after I told her about Alex's offer. "It would solve all the money problems. Do you think Alex would keep any of your employees? Maybe give us a raise?"

"No Angie, you don't get it. I don't want to sell. Besides, the guy is dangerous. I wouldn't want you or anyone else to work for him." I'd decided I needed to warn the staff about the situation. I should have guessed Angie would focus on the money.

"But Beri, don't you realize how bad our finances are? There's not much time to turn things around. Two of our planes are out of operation. Who knows when our insurance will reimburse us or how high our premiums will go? Besides, winter is almost here. Work will slow down soon. This could be the answer to your prayers."

"That man's not the answer to *anyone's* prayers," I said with emphasis. "Stay as far away from him as you can."

Ross walked through the door from the hangar. "Not talking about me, I hope?" he said with a smile.

He reached my desk and tipped my chair slightly. "How about driving over to my office for a minute? I have something I want to show you."

"Let me grab my jacket."

"Just when the conversation was getting interesting," Angie muttered.

The tiny cubicle of Ross' office was tucked into a corner of his hangar. He ushered me in and closed the door behind us, pulling out a chair for me.

"What's up?" I asked.

He handed me a letter with FAA letterhead. "Remember when I told you about this? My suspicions were right on."

The paper was a notification of an incident review involving his student disregarding his instructions with the tower. "Uh oh."

"I'm not particularly worried. It just confirms my impression."

I met his eyes. "If I were you, I'd take it seriously. I know my FAA hearing turned out to be a bigger ordeal than I expected, and they don't seem to be in any hurry to review the new evidence Dean turned up."

Ross nodded. "I'll keep that in mind. I have a couple of weeks to think about it."

He got up and opened a miniature refrigerator in the corner. "Want something to drink before we get to the real reason I wanted to talk?"

"The real reason?" I leaned forward to see what he had to offer. "Have any diet soda in there?"

He handed me a diet Coke and opened an energy drink for himself. "How did it go when you talked to the police? I've been worried about your safety."

"They took the report. That was about it. I also talked to an FBI agent acquaintance of mine earlier today. He seemed more interested than the police, and I did learn a few things from him."

"Oh? Like what?"

"Like how he's familiar with Alex Veronin. Said his company is suspected of having roots in organized crime. And, he thinks you may be right about Veronin wanting to force us out. Cartos may want space on Merrill Field to run a money laundering operation. He said aviation offers some advantages for that kind of thing."

"Huh. Who'd have thought they'd want to move into Alaska? For that matter, I haven't heard much about organized crime in California. Guess I thought it mostly an East Coast thing."

"It's everywhere. Anyway, Jack's with Dennis now. It hurt to send him, but he wanted to go, and I wanted him to stay safe."

"You made a good decision under the circumstances." He covered my hand with his. "When does your dad return?"

"Another couple of days?" I shrugged. "At least that's my best guess. I'm not able to reach him by phone."

"In the meantime, do you want to stay at your place or mine? I don't think you should be alone. Veronin may decide to get nasty."

"I'm a big girl, and I won't be alone. I have Tiger."

Ross laughed. "Big help he'd be. He might scare an intruder, but only one who walked into his wagging tail."

"Puhleese. He's a good guard dog."

"Be sensible, Beri. I care about you. Let me sleep on your sofa or you can sleep on mine, but you can't afford to take any chances staying alone. Jack would never forgive me if anything happened to you." He let go of my hand. "I'll meet you at your house at six. I'll bring my toothbrush and a pizza."

Ross and I arrived at the house about the same time. He emerged from his Jeep with a large pizza box as I pushed the garage door opener and drove up the driveway. He loped inside the garage to meet me.

After I closed the garage door, he held out his hand to stop me. "Hold on. Let me go in and check things out first."

"Hey, I'm not in the Witness Protection Program. Let's not get carried away here."

Ross frowned, but went inside. The house was silent. "Don't you think it's strange that Tiger isn't greeting us at the door?"

"Now that you mention it, yes. Maybe he went out back through the doggie door."

"Don't call him yet. Let's look around first." Ross pulled a Beretta from his backpack, and we went room to room checking things out. No burglar. No Tiger.

"Well, I guess we can yell 'clear' now," I said. "Let me check outside for Tiger."

We walked together around the side of the house to the dog run. Tiger lay sprawled inside, whimpering. When he saw us, his tail thumped once, a lackluster attempt compared to his usual vigorous wags.

"Tiger!" I opened the gate, knelt down and placed his head in my lap. "Are you okay, boy?"

The dog struggled to get up and gave my face a lick.

"Good boy," I said. "What happened to you? Did someone hurt you?"

Ross ran his hands over Tiger's body. "Aha!" he said pointing to two small punctures on the dog's shoulder. "I think he was tasered."

"But why, if they didn't break in?"

"Who knows, maybe they intended to go inside but changed their mind. Or maybe they're sending you a message."

Tiger was standing now, so we took him inside. I phoned the vet to see if we should bring him in, but was told to keep him quiet and watch him. Tiger walked around the den once and sniffed the pizza box on the table. He then curled up in his bed and went to sleep.

Halfway through eating our pizza, my phone rang. It was Jack's coach.

"Hi Beri. Have you heard from Jack since he left?"

"He called when he arrived in Arizona. Said the flight went well, and he's anxious to leave for Germany. He sounded happy to see his dad."

"Glad to hear it. I called to tell you about something odd that happened at practice today. Probably nothing, but I thought you should know a couple of guys came by asking questions about Jack."

I backed against the wall, feeling faint "Really?" I croaked, as I reached for my locket. "What kind of questions?"

"They asked which boy was Jack, if this was the team he played on? That kind of thing. I didn't tell them where he was. Just said he wasn't playing today."

"Can you describe them?"

"Tall, well-built, early thirties, wearing baseball caps. One had long, curly blond hair. The other had darker hair and a soul patch. Nothing especially remarkable about them, but the one who spoke to me did have an accent. I think it was Russian."

"I appreciate the call. Thanks for the heads-up. I'm sorry I had to pull Jack off the team."

"Don't worry about it. Maybe he can play again next year."

I clicked the phone off and turned to Ross. "I think you're right. They're trying to scare me, and it's working. First Tiger and now Jack's baseball team. I'm so glad he's not here. Tomorrow I'll call Alex Veronin and tell him I absolutely will not sell the company. He can focus his energies somewhere else."

"You realize that will probably make things worse."

"I don't care. This whole situation is ridiculous. I'm also going to have cameras installed at the house and at the office. If he sends his goons again, at least I'll have evidence."

Ross started cleaning up the pizza mess. "I'll save a piece for Tiger when he wakes up. He deserves it."

The next morning, I woke and started the coffee. Tiger whined at the door to go outside rather than going out the dog door to his run like he usually did. I let him out and was cooking eggs when Ross emerged from Jack's bedroom.

"Strange waking up to a wall of bird photos staring at me," Ross said. "Wasn't sure where I was for a minute. Thought I might be in the rain forest."

I laughed. "Hope you slept well." I pulled a couple of plates from the cupboard. "Scrambled okay?"

"Sounds good." He took the plate I handed him. "Did I hear the garage door open?"

I looked up to see Dad as he walked through the kitchen door and tossed a newspaper on the table.

"Hey Dad. Glad you're home! I didn't expect you so soon."

"I can see that," he said, with a sour expression on his face. "I see I'm interrupting something." He dropped his duffel bag beside the stairs. "Hello Ross. Call me old-fashioned, but I'd say you're moving awfully fast."

"Wait a minute, Dad. I don't want you to have the wrong impression," I said. "Ross slept in Jack's room last night because things have been tense since you've been gone. He didn't want me to be here alone, that's all."

"Uh huh." Dad started up the stairs. "Where's Jack if Ross slept in his bed?"

"Jack left to go on vacation with Dennis. It's a long story. Why don't you sit down and have some breakfast, and we'll fill you in."

Dad reversed course. "No need. I can't believe you'd send Jack off after we'd agreed you wouldn't." He hoisted the duffel bag to his shoulder and carried it to the door. "I need to dry out my camping gear. I'll sleep in my tent tonight and give you lovebirds your privacy."

Ross jumped up. "I can see I'm not needed. I'll be going now."

"Don't rush off. I'm already leaving." Dad let the garage door slam behind him.

"Sorry we upset him," Ross said to me. "Just promise me you'll explain to him that you're in danger."

"Of course I will. It's the only way he'll forgive me for sending Jack to stay with Dennis. I just hope I can convince Dad we're not a couple."

"Oh, I don't know. Wouldn't it be simpler just to fulfill his expectations?"

I threw the newspaper at him in reply.

Chapter Twenty-six

Dad hammered the last tent stake into the ground as I joined him outside. "Dad, let's talk. I don't want us to be upset with each other. I think you'll understand if you'll let me explain what's been going on."

"I think you've explained enough already." He gave me a sidelong glance and a mule-headed shake of his head.

Grabbing a couple of folding chairs from the garage, I sat down across from him. "I know you didn't want Jack to leave. I didn't either, but I agreed to send him because I was worried about his safety."

"Safety? He'd be safer traipsing around Europe than staying home with us?"

"Normally no, but Veronin recently made threats against me and our family."

"And you believe them?"

"I wasn't sure at first, but yesterday Jack's coach called to tell me two guys were at the ball park asking about Jack.

"Who were they?"

"I don't know, but the coach didn't recognize them, and he mentioned they spoke with a Russian accent."

"So you think they were Veronin's henchmen?"

"I don't know for sure, but I suspect they were. And another thing, Last night, someone tasered Tiger here at the house before I got home."

Dad's eyes softened. "Tiger? Is he okay?"

"Yes, he seems his usual self. The vet thought he'd be fine. No visible damage to him."

I wanted Dad's advice, and it was a relief to share the details with him. "Do you remember me telling you about Cartos sub-contracting several large mapping projects to us earlier this year?"

I saw Dad nod so I went on. "Well now, they want to buy the company, and Veronin's not giving me a choice. He's told me if I don't sell, I'll regret it."

"How? Did he say?"

"I don't know exactly. I took it as a threat when he brought up my family."

"Is he offering a fair price?"

"Yes. That's not the problem. I just don't want to sell, and I don't like his strong-arm tactics."

"How much?" he asked.

"He's up to six million."

"*What?* You turned it down? The business isn't worth that much."

"I know, but I didn't want Jack in the crosshairs."

"Why won't you sell?"

I put my hand on his arm. "Because I love what I do, Dad, and I love that you built this business. Because the employees depend on me, and because I don't want the mob to strong-arm me."

"The mob? What do you mean?"

"An FBI contact of mine tells me that Cartos is connected to organized crime."

"If that's true, there's even more reason not to cross them. What are you thinking?" He took his hat off and tossed it on the ground.

"Dad, come on. I've never known you to walk away from a fight."

"Maybe not, but you've never known me to throw rocks at a bee hive, either."

"I'll be careful, but I want you to be, too." I gave him a hug. "Don't be surprised when workmen come later this morning to install the security cameras I ordered." I stood to leave. "I'd better be getting to work."

"Hold on just a minute. It's Saturday, so the bank won't be open." He handed me a heavy leather poke. "I deposited the bulk of my stake in the bank in Nome, but can you put my nuggets in the office safe until Monday? I'm saving them for Jack's college fund."

"Sure thing," I said, taking the pouch. "You'll come back in the house now that Ross is gone, won't you?"

"No, I think I'll stay out here a while longer. I like the fresh air," he said settling down in his chair. "Don't start thinking you've convinced me you're doing the right thing. I think your stubbornness is putting your life in danger and throwing away a fortune at the same time."

"Seems to me that stubbornness runs in our gene pool."

I left and thought about Dad's words while I drove to work. Why was I so determined to hang on to the business? The reasons I gave Dad were all true, but I would never forgive myself if someone got hurt because I insisted on thwarting Alex and his plans. Was I being unreasonable? What was the worst thing that could happen if I did sell it? *Just the end of life as I know it.* The life I wanted to continue living. I didn't want to lose it. I wanted things to stay the same.

I bit my lip. No, I had to stand up to Veronin. If everyone caved to his kind of pressure, crime would take over everything. I'd already let his deadline pass, but I'd call him this morning and officially refuse his offer.

It turned out it wasn't that simple. I called Alex's cell phone, but got no answer. It wasn't possible to leave a message because his voice mailbox was full. When I talked to the hotel staff, I was told he'd already checked out. Finally, I called the main number for Cartos in California and left a message for him there.

It wasn't a good morning for phone calls. When I tried to reach Paige Abbott to check on her progress with the photos, I reached her answering machine. I wondered if she was out of town again or was trying to avoid me until she had money to pay her bill. I left a message asking her to call me.

I powered up my computer and decided to screen the latest photos I'd taken. I didn't have much confidence in the Rainy Pass pictures I'd given Paige now that I thought I knew Ken's actual destination. The last pictures taken of the new location held the most promise. I scrolled through frame after frame until the work grew tedious, my shoulder muscles stiff. Just as I was about to give up, I noticed several small planes parked haphazardly around a large rectangular building near a small lake. The location was remote with no sign of another development near it. Curious, but probably not suspicious.

Frustrated, I tried to think of another angle to pursue. I remembered Vic mentioning a pilot who had also experienced problems with mislabeled parts. I picked up the phone and called him.

"Hey Vic. This is Beri."

"Howdy. How's life in the big city?"

"Fine. I'm calling to ask if you've heard of any more problems with bad airplane parts." I drummed my fingers on the desk as I waited.

"No, not really. I did talk to the pilot I mentioned. He said he'd stopped buying his parts locally. He gets them online now and hasn't had any more difficulties. In his opinion, someone in Alaska is recycling parts from crashed airplanes. They wouldn't be FAA approved and he doesn't trust them to be safe."

"Thanks. Please let me know if you hear anything else."

"Will do." Vic paused. "Oh Beri, one more thing. He also said he suspects an outfit in the Lake Iliamna area might be running a chop shop."

"Stolen cars?"

"Funny. No, stolen planes."

"Can you find out exactly where?"

"I'll try, but I don't know when I'll see the guy again."

Interesting. Maybe I should check out that establishment I'd spotted on my photo. It could be a possibility at least.

I spent the rest of the afternoon writing proposals for advertised aerial photography projects. I even responded to requests from other states if they could be flown during winter months. Business slows down in Alaska when snow is on the ground, but one advantage of using airplanes in my line of work is that I could go where the work is.

Sunday morning, I was in the office alone with the doors locked. I continued working on proposals. Landing a big project or two was my best chance for financial survival. I spotted several good possibilities, but each would require a lot of time to complete the required paperwork. I made a list of the financial documents and bonding certificates I'd need so I could delegate those to Angie.

Hearing a car drive up outside, I tried to see who it was from the window. No luck, it had parked too far around the edge of the building. A few minutes later, someone started pounding on the office door.

I pulled my survival gun from the desk drawer where I'd recently stashed it and went to the door. No use taking any chances.

"Who's there?" I asked.

"I have a message for you from Mr. Veronin," a masculine voice said.

"Go ahead with it. I'm all ears."

"No. Open the door, or we'll open it ourselves and maybe smash a couple of airplanes, too."

Uh oh. I picked up the phone and called 9-1-1.

"Someone is threatening to break down my door. I have reason to fear for my life. Please hurry," I whispered. I left the line open and had just put the phone down when the pounding on the door began again.

"Lady, I'm not fooling here. Are you going to let me in or not?"

"I'll open the door, but you should know the police are on their way."

"Yeah, whatever. I'm going to count to five and then I'm going to start smashing."

"Okay, already. I'm unlocking it now." I pulled the door open and stood aside, holding my Smith and Wesson ready to fire.

Two tall muscular men burst in toward me. They matched the descriptions of the guys at the ballpark. They took one look at my gun and stopped short.

"Shit! Do you even know how to use that?" the blond one asked.

"Sure do. I've won three marksmanship championships."

"Drop it, Miss, or I'll shoot you." He pulled a Glock from his hip and raised it in my direction.

I fired, hitting him in the wrist.

He dropped the gun shrieking, and grabbed his arm.

"I can't believe you shot me," his partner said, moving his hand toward his pocket.

"Wouldn't do that if I were you," I said, swinging my gun in his direction. "Hear those sirens? I'm sure they're coming on account of you."

"C'mon," he said, grabbing the good arm of his injured companion. "Let's get out of here." He bent to pick up the fallen gun.

"Leave it or I'll shoot you, too!"

They left. I relocked the door and moved away from the windows. I waited in the classroom until I heard the police roll up outside. My legs were weak. True, I knew how to shoot, but I'd never shot a person before. I'd gambled, aiming for his hand instead of a bigger target, but it was the best I could bring myself to do. Glad my aim was good.

I let the officers inside, anxious to encourage them to find the thugs before they got too far away. They stared at the blood and the gun on the floor and asked what happened.

"Two men burst in the door after threatening to break it down if I didn't open it. One pointed the Glock at me and threatened to shoot. I shot him instead."

"Judging from the amount of blood, you winged him good. What did you shoot him with?"

I pointed to my desk drawer. "My gun is in there if you want to check it."

He pulled the drawer open and took the gun out with his gloved hand. "Geez, no wonder there's a lot of blood. Where was he hit?"

"In the wrist or maybe the hand. He dropped his gun anyway."

"No kidding. Can you describe these guys?"

I started to describe the men, then remembered the cameras. "I had security cameras installed earlier today. You can check them. I didn't see their vehicle, but it might show up on the camera footage. If you leave soon you might catch them."

"Do you know why they were here?" asked the taller of the two officers.

"No, but I have a good idea who they are. I think they're henchmen working for Alex Veronin. He recently threatened me if I didn't sell my business to him. He gave me a deadline which has since passed."

"Wasn't there a murder here recently?" the shorter policeman asked.

"Yes. Our intern, Buzz. He was a student at the university. His memorial service is scheduled tomorrow."

"Any connection to these guys?"

I shrugged. "I have no idea why they'd want to kill Buzz, and I hadn't received any threats before that happened. I don't know if there's a connection."

"We'll let the crime scene folks get to work here. We'll need you to come down to the station with us."

"Is that necessary? Can't we do it here?" I asked. "I really hate to leave the office unguarded."

"Sorry, but shots were fired. Besides, I think you need to hire security guards for your office. This doesn't appear to be something you should handle yourself."

"But…don't you need to go after the guys that threatened me?"

"I'll have an officer check the hospitals, but those guys are probably long gone by now."

I tried to calm down while I grabbed my purse and jacket and accompanied the officers out. This was getting to be one headache after another, and I was getting exasperated.

Chapter Twenty-seven

The police gave me the number of a security guard service. I arranged for twenty-four-hour armed guard coverage with a short-term contract, I hoped we wouldn't need to renew.

After giving my statement at the police station, I went home knowing I'd need some sleep before attending the memorial service in the morning. Buzz's parents had notified us that it would be held at the university auditorium at ten. We'd already made plans to close the office so everyone could attend. I reminded myself to call the security guard service and notify them of this as I had forgotten to mention it when I signed the contract.

Dad's tent was still in the yard, but he was sitting in the kitchen eating a stack of pancakes when I walked in.

"Keeping late hours?" he asked.

"Not by choice. I've been at the police station. A couple of miscreants tried to break in, and I had to shoot one of them after he pulled a gun."

He put down his coffee mug, sloshing a small puddle on the table. "Did you kill him?" he asked.

"No, just shot the gun out of his hand."

"That's my girl. Did the police arrest them?"

"Not yet, but I think they will soon. The cameras got clear shots of them."

"Good timing putting those in. Don't know if you noticed, but they finished installing the cameras here, too."

"Good. I also hired security guards for the office. I can't take a chance on the staff being attacked again or our planes being damaged."

"Sounds expensive."

"Yes, but necessary. I should probably do the same here at the house. I'm not sure the cameras will be enough."

"Nah. I'll be here. I wouldn't worry about it."

"I definitely feel better now that you're back, but be careful." I gazed out the window. "I assume you're going to take the tent down?"

"I don't think so. I can stand guard better out there, and Tiger will alert me if anyone tries to prowl around while we're outside."

"Dad, you're too exposed out there."

"I'll be fine, but it might be a good idea to invite your boyfriend to stay inside with you at night."

"He's not my boyfriend, but I'll ask Ross. At this point, we can't be too careful."

More than a hundred people attended the memorial service for Buzz the next morning. The family shared a montage of slides portraying Buzz's activities beginning in childhood and continuing until the present year. He appeared vibrant and happy in the pictures, and close to his family. Several students told humorous stories about Buzz and his exploits, and a professor praised his ambition and dedication to his studies.

Dean surprised me when he walked to the front of the room. He stood for a moment in silence, then spoke quietly. "Buzz treated everyone with respect. He worked hard and learned all he could. Buzz was a friend to everyone. He was a boy, but he lived like a man." He lowered his head for a moment and left the podium.

Somehow Dean's simple eulogy conveyed a poignancy even more potent than the others. Perhaps it was because I knew how heartfelt his words were. The program ended, my throat constricted to half its usual size. I gave my condolences to the family and left.

Dean and the rest of the staff left a few minutes before I did. I'd just started toward the parking lot when I saw Ross walking ahead of me. I increased my pace to catch up with him. "Ross, wait. I didn't see you inside."

He reversed course and joined me. "I'm not surprised. That was quite a crowd." Ross gave me a hug. "How are you holding up? I just heard about the break-in."

"I'm okay." My voice caught and I shivered. "Just sad. First Ken and then

Buzz. Both are such a loss. They were so young."

Ross gave me a hug. "It's hard to comprehend, that's for sure."

"All I know is that the creeps who shot Buzz have to be caught." I clenched my jaw. "I've got to figure out who did it and why."

"Have the police made any progress?"

"If they have, they aren't talking. I'm beginning to wonder if it's all connected to Cartos. Speaking of which, Dad suggested I ask you if you'd be willing to sleep at the house for a few nights until things have settled down. I hired security guards for the office, but can't afford them for the house."

"Your Dad asked, huh?"

"Yes. Hard to believe, but he did."

Ross stopped in his tracks. "And how about you? Are you asking?" A smile played on his lips.

"I am," I said, keeping my voice level. "I would appreciate it very much."

I returned to the office to finish my paperwork. Ross picked me up afterwards and we left my car at the office and drove home together. I sensed something was wrong the moment I spotted Dad's camping gear scattered across the yard. It wasn't like Dad to be so disorganized with his gear. I jumped out of the car and ran toward the semi-collapsed tent, Ross following close behind.

"Oh my God!" Dad's feet, toe side down, protruded from one side of the partially collapsed tent. A bloody baseball bat rested against one foot.

"Dad?"

No response.

I pulled the tent off him and found him lying on his stomach with blood oozing from a wound on his head.

Ross dialed 9-1-1 and requested an ambulance.

"Dad, can you hear me?" I asked, kneeling down beside him.

He moaned and tried to sit up.

"No, stay still. The paramedics are on their way." I found a blanket and covered him while I searched for something to stop the bleeding. Not finding a towel, I pulled a white t-shirt from Dad's duffle and carefully held it to the wound with one hand.

Tiger crawled out from under what was left of the tent and whined. He licked Dad's face and lay down beside him.

"He hit…" Dad shuddered, his eyes rolled back and he lost consciousness.

I clung to his hand with my other hand. He didn't look good. It was clear he'd lost a lot of blood. He couldn't just fade away. I sobbed with relief when I heard the squall of sirens.

A moment later, Ross walked out to direct the wave of the police cars into the driveway. He assured them the attacker was gone, but the police thoroughly checked the area before allowing the paramedics and fire truck to roll in.

I gave what information I could to the paramedics and answered questions for the police officers. I assured them I wasn't at home at the time of the attack and had not seen the attacker.

The paramedics loaded Dad into the ambulance. I started to climb in behind him, but was stopped by the lead paramedic.

"Sorry, Miss. You'll have to meet us at the hospital. We're going to be busy keeping him stable. We'll take him to Providence Hospital. It's closest."

Ross steered me to his Jeep and lifted Tiger inside. "I'll drive so you can call the vet and explain things. We'll drop Tiger off on our way to the ER. He seems woozy and he may be injured, too."

I nodded and got into the vehicle on auto-pilot. As the ambulance left, siren and lights flashing, I crumbled. I felt Ross' arms encircle me and I leaned back into him. My only thought was how relieved I was that Jack wasn't here.

Chapter Twenty-eight

The next morning Ross drove me home from the hospital. Dad remained unconscious, but his doctor and the nursing staff considered his condition stable. I thought about calling Jack, but I didn't want him to worry. Dad wouldn't have wanted that, either. We stopped to pick up Tiger from the veterinary clinic on the way.

"How is he?" I asked the vet when we arrived.

"He's a trooper. He's doing just fine." She handed me his leash. "Keep him quiet and near you. I don't doubt he was traumatized by the attack, but he doesn't appear to be physically hurt."

"Thanks, Doc. I think we're both going to take it easy today."

As soon as we arrived at the house, Tiger jumped from the car and walked stiff-legged over to what was left of Dad's campsite. He tracked around the perimeter, hackles raised along his spine and tail motionless.

"C'mon boy, Dad will recover and come home soon. Let's go inside." I patted his head and led him up the steps to the front door.

Ross walked ahead of me. "Wait here while I walk through the house."

"If anyone is here, Tiger will let us know."

Ross touched Tiger's shoulder. "Okay then. Let's check things out, boy."

They circled through the rooms and returned to the kitchen where I was sitting. Ross patted my shoulder. "Don't be so glum. Everything is going to be fine."

I smiled at him. I know, but I feel so guilty leaving Dad at the hospital alone."

"You've done all you can until they wake him up. Keeping him in a coma will limit the swelling in his brain. It's the best thing for him."

"Maybe, but it kills me to think about him lying there alone with tubes sprouting in all directions. I need to be there when he wakes up."

"You will be. For now, though, you need to take care of yourself and get some decent rest."

"First, I've got to go through Dad's paperwork and figure out what kind of health insurance he has. The hospital insisted they needed the information immediately. I have no idea since I don't think he ever went to see a doctor."

"Didn't he have an insurance card in his wallet?"

"The police didn't find his wallet. Apparently whoever attacked him, robbed him. I think he keeps all his paperwork in a file box in the top of his closet. If I know him, he just tosses everything inside. It's probably going to take a while."

"I'll help you get the box down," Ross said. "If you like, I can go through things with you."

I nodded. "Thanks."

Dad's closet was stuffed with bags, boxes, boots and a few clothes. After a bit of rummaging, I located the box in one corner, and Ross pulled it down.

We sat on the bed and opened the lid. Off to the side, I spotted a group of envelopes held together with a rubber band. Maybe this wouldn't be as bad as I'd thought. I pulled out the top envelope and noticed the six-cent postage stamp and postmark of April, 1970. Not what I needed. I replaced the envelope and put the packet aside.

"You're right about the disorganization," Ross said. "There are statements in here from years ago mixed in with others from last month."

"He always says he's allergic to paperwork. It's an unfortunate trait I'm afraid I've inherited, which is one reason why I hired Angie."

Ross grabbed a handful of paper. "I'll work on this pile."

I started sifting through loose papers and eventually held one up. "Here's something. It's a bill from an AARP supplemental policy."

"Great. If he had that, he must have Medicare," Ross said. "Aha, here it is. This should do it."

"He's busted. I *knew* he wasn't fifty-nine, but I didn't know he was *over* sixty-five." I dumped a load of paper into the file box, keeping the Medicare and insurance papers aside. At the last minute, I pulled out the stack of old letters, thinking they might be interesting to read later.

Ross closed the box and returned it to its place in the closet.

I took the packet of letters downstairs with me. They were old enough that it didn't feel like I was invading Dad's privacy, especially since they were from my grandmother. Besides, they made me feel close to him somehow.

I sat at the kitchen table and put them in sequential order by postmark with the oldest on top. Most of them appeared to have been sent to him while he was in the military. The first couple were chatty notes keeping him updated on residents of the small town in Washington where he'd grown up. I skimmed them, recognizing only a few names. The third one got my attention. Uncle Harold had died, Gram wrote. He'd named Dad and his cousin Thomas (Ace) Hanratty in his will. Since they were both stationed overseas, the attorney notified Aunt Rita and Gram to represent their sons at the reading of the will. He'd be sending release forms for the cousins to sign.

The final letter from Gram related the terms of the will which included leaving gold claims in Alaska to the two cousins. Instructions on actions they would need to take to maintain the claims were attached to her letter.

> *I hope you don't get too excited about this and decide to become a gold miner instead of going back to school when you get out, she wrote to Dad. Aunt Rita is so afraid Thomas will be bitten by the gold bug that she's not even telling him about all this. He'll have to figure it out for himself from what the attorney sends him.*

The remaining envelopes contained paperwork Dad had filed with the state regarding his maintenance of his claims. A final envelope was a diatribe from Ace Hanratty, furious that Dad hadn't told him what he needed to do to retain his claims. Apparently, because he hadn't kept them up, they had reverted to the government and had been included in the Native Claims Settlement. He'd lost all chance of reclaiming them, and he blamed Dad for it, not his mother.

Ross left after admonishing me to stay inside and keep all the doors locked, saying he was going to clean up Dad's stuff from the front yard and then head home for a change of clothes. I followed orders for a while and even tried to take a nap. My head swam with worries about Dad, and confusion about what had happened to him. My eyes wouldn't stay closed. Plus, I wanted to talk to Ace about the letters I'd read.

Tiger seemed to feel as edgy as I did, so I didn't want to leave him alone. I snapped his leash on his collar and led him out to the car. "Want to take a drive with me, boy?" He jumped in without hesitation and relaxed on the seat beside me.

I parked outside Hanratty's and opened the car door to get out. Tiger stood and walked across the seat to follow.

"I guess you can come with me, boy. We shouldn't be long." I led him inside the building. The bell jangled on the front door bringing Ace to the counter.

Tiger yelped and began a low rumbling growl, his teeth bared.

"Get that cur out of here," Ace shouted. "No animals allowed."

"I'll put him in the car. There's something I want to talk to you about."

"It'll have to wait. I was just getting ready to leave."

"It'll just take a minute."

"I said *get out!*"

"Fine. I'm leaving."

After putting the car in reverse to leave the parking lot, I turned to Tiger. "What was that all about, boy? I take it you don't like him."

I'd never seen Tiger react that way before, but then again, I didn't recall him ever being around Ace. Still, it made me wonder what had gotten into Tiger.

Chapter Twenty-nine

The next morning, I sat with Dad for an hour watching his monitors blink out blips and numbers I didn't understand. Finally, I decided I needed to get to work. I gave him a kiss on the cheek and left.

When I walked into the office, Angie jumped up and hugged me.

"Beri, I'm so sorry to hear about your Dad. How is he doing?"

I did a half-shrug with one shoulder. "About as well as can be expected, the doctors say. We just have to wait it out and pray he'll come through unscathed."

"Such a thing. Who would have thought he could be attacked in his own front yard? Did your security camera show who did it?"

I hit my forehead with the palm of my hand. I'd been so upset when I'd found Dad, I'd forgotten to mention my newly installed security system to the police. Angie had a point. Maybe the culprit could be identified. "Thanks, Angie! I'm going home to check the camera and I'll let the police know if it shows anything."

"They didn't notice it?"

"Not that I know of. I'll be in touch."

Once home, I jumped out of my car and ran to the front of the house to where the camera had been mounted under the eave of the roof. I spotted the bracket, but not the camera. Smashed black plastic and glass littered the ground below. The person responsible must have spotted it and destroyed it. But when? Before or after the attack?

I made a quick call to the security company. They assured me any footage would be recoverable from the hard drive. All their data was forwarded in real time. I could check with them tomorrow. I thanked them and asked them to forward anything they found to the police as soon as possible.

Back at work, I walked by Angie's desk. She leaned over, picked up an envelope and handed it to me. "Glad to see you. I signed for this while you were out. It came certified mail. Did you learn anything about the attackers?"

"No, not yet." I glanced at the address. "It's from the FAA." Uh oh.

I tore it open and pulled out a single sheet of paper. "I don't believe this! It's a notice of suspension of my license pending a final hearing scheduled next week. I'll be out of business if they do this."

"Can't you stop it?"

"I won't give up without a fight, you can count on that." I threw the notice on my desk, sat down and picked up the phone. "I already have an appointment with an aviation attorney. I need to see if I can move it up to see him today."

I walked out of the attorney's office confused. He couldn't understand the reasoning behind the FAA's action any more than I could. I reviewed our conversation in my head.

"Didn't you share the fuel contamination evidence with them?" he'd asked.

"Of course we did. My mechanic went over it with them in detail."

"Something's not right. Let's check with the NTSB and see what they have to say about the cause of the crash. I'll take care of that. I have some contacts there," he'd said.

At least for now, I could still fly. No telling if that would still be true next week. I'd best make good use of the time I had.

I grabbed the stack of photos I'd printed of the new search area as soon as I got back to the office. I flipped through them until I came to the series including the isolated building near a small lake. Eight parked planes surrounded the building. I noticed several of them were Super Cubs similar to the plane Ken was flying. Not much of a lead, but it was worth checking. I filled Angie in on my plans, gathered my gear and jogged out to my plane.

Visibility was good with a forecast of light overcast and possible showers later in the day. Not good enough for photography, but fine for my purposes today. I'd keep an eye on any changes as the day progressed.

Once in the air, I relaxed for the first time since opening the FAA notice. It was a beautiful day for flying, and I felt a ray of optimism. My attorney would handle his end. In the meantime, I had to try to figure out what was going on and learn what happened to Ken.

Almost two hours later, a few passes over the outpost piqued my curiosity even more than before. None of the Cubs tied down outside had tail numbers. This was odd because these numbers are required by the government before a plane can be flown. Were these planes here to be repainted? I decided to land and ask a few questions. Maybe inquire about having my plane painted. I figured I should let the office know my plans, but unsurprisingly found no cell phone coverage available.

As I circled the compound, I checked the wind sock for wind direction, and noticed a Super Cub on floats docked behind the buildings. I landed on the dirt strip and taxied toward the hangar. No sooner had I cut the engine than a large heavy-set man charged toward me, his face twisted in a scowl.

"What do you think you're doing here?" he shouted.

I opened the door and hopped out of my plane. "Just stopped by. It appears you have some kind of repair shop here and I need to get my plane painted. Thought I'd check your prices."

"Yeah, sure." He turned to another man who had emerged from the building, a thin, sallow fellow with black-framed eyeglasses. "Be careful of this bitch. She could be dangerous."

"Please. Do I look dangerous?" I held my hands out to my side. "Like I said, I'm just passing by."

"Sure you are. Help me take her inside, Pete. We'll keep her there until we find out what the boss wants to do with her."

"Hey, that's uncalled for!" I tried to evade their grasp. I hadn't expected this level of resistance. Why were they being so hostile?

Half-carrying, half-pushing me to the hangar, the two men bound my hands behind my back and left me sitting on the floor of the hangar tied to a large concrete tie-down block. I could hear the men talking outside, but couldn't make out their words.

The hangar was spacious and well organized. *How was I going to get out of this?* I surveyed my surroundings and noticed a new Cub parked at the far end of the building, its cowling open. A red Craftsman tool chest on wheels stood nearby. A large cluttered work bench covered most of one wall, a case of oil pushed underneath. A compressor sat nearby next to a couple of acetylene tanks for welding and a small band saw. A metal press for bending metal stood near the door, and boxes of various airplane parts were stacked in a corner.

The voices outside grew closer. I heard a squawking noise. One of the men was talking on a radio.

"Yessir. She's secure. No worries there. Uh huh. All right, I'll get him out of here. We should be there in about 40 minutes."

The big guy opened the door and walked over to me. He rechecked my restraints and gave me a kick in the thigh. "Not going anywhere, are you?" He laughed and left, the door clanging shut behind him.

A few minutes later, I heard what sounded like the engine and prop of a Cessna 180 roar to life. Were they leaving me here alone or were there others somewhere on the premises?

After about five minutes of silence, I tried lifting the tie-down block by the re-bar loops on top. It felt awkward and much too heavy to lift with my hands tied behind my back. I tried dragging the concrete anchor and found I could move it a few inches. Time to decide which direction I wanted to go. It was too painful a process to change my mind midway.

I spotted a rippled washboard-like piece of metal against one wall. At least I could reach it from the floor.

I inch-wormed my way across the floor slowly, hoping I'd reach my destination before the men returned.

Exhausted, I finally drew near. I rested a moment, giving my wrists, raw from the effort, a chance to recuperate.

Backing up to a metal edge, I found I couldn't get my ropes close enough to do any good. I stood as best I could in an inverted "U" position, tilting the block so the rope could be abraded by the bent metal. I rocked back and forth. If my wrists didn't give out my spine likely would, but I persevered until I felt a strand of rope loosen and give way.

My heart leaped. Finally, I was making progress.

I sawed with increased ferocity, and a few minutes later I broke free. I collapsed and lay prone on the floor, wiping the blood from my wrists with my shirt.

Examining the metal contraption that had saved me, I noticed lettering stenciled along one side. *Property of Ken Abbott*. It was part of Ken's prospecting equipment! Could he have been captured, too?

I had to find out, but how? If my captors returned now, one glance inside the hangar and I'd be exposed. I needed help and fast.

I cracked the hangar door open slightly and peered out without seeing anyone. My Super Cub was still parked near the hangar where I'd left it. I regretted I hadn't taken a faster plane with a bigger fuel capacity. I would need to refuel to make it to Anchorage and I didn't think there was a fuel station nearby.

I walked around the plane and spotted the fabric of my plane's tail—slashed. Grounded. The plane was not airworthy. I couldn't control the elevators.

Now what?

The remaining planes appeared to be stripped and inoperable. If the plane Ken flew was here, I couldn't identify it without closer inspection. I slipped back into the hangar to check the plane parked there.

I lifted the cowling and found everything appeared intact, then climbed into the cockpit and checked inside. The interior had that "new plane smell". My eye fell on something familiar. A Ninety-Nines Club decal decorated a side window. I recognized it as similar to the one in the catalog I'd seen at the recent Ninety-Nines meeting. Was this Kaitlin's stolen plane and could I use it to escape? I'm sure she would be delighted if I returned it to its rightful owner.

I climbed out on a strut, twisted off the gas cap and checked inside. I couldn't see any fuel. Hopping down, I ran over to the work bench to find a fuel stick. I grabbed one, climbed back on the plane and checked the gas levels in the wings. Both sides were almost empty. No time to fill the tanks even assuming I could find fuel, and there was no way I could refuel the plane without being seen. If anyone returned, I'd be a sitting duck. What next?

Only one possibility remained.

The float plane.

I slid out of the hangar, taking Ken's sluice and some rope with me. I could use it as proof he'd been here when I contacted the authorities. The lake was 100 feet away.

I dragged the sluice along a path cut into the grass until I reached the beach and the small dock where the plane was tied. This had to work. The plane was an older model Cub that had been in frequent use. I tied the sluice to the strut under one wing and tested it to make certain it was secure.

After a rapid preflight check, everything appeared to be in the green with fuel in both tanks. I suspected this plane served as a workhorse for the men working here. I flipped the magneto and master switches, took a deep breath and pushed the starter button. The engine fired up. I felt a rush of relief, taxied to the end of the lake, pushed the throttle forward to get up on step and took off into the wind.

I didn't see anyone on the ground to notice me leave. After climbing to altitude, I flew towards Anchorage. I checked the fuel gauge. Enough to get part way. I'd need to make a refueling stop in Kenai.

A few minutes out, I spotted a Cessna 180 heading toward me. *Crap!*

It was one of my captors returning. The plane turned in my direction and rapidly closed the distance between us. I had by far the slower plane. While float planes have their advantages, speed isn't one of them. Floats cause too much drag.

The plane chasing me drew close enough I could see the pilot alone inside. He dropped behind me, but stayed close. I jerked in surprise as a spider web spread across the plexiglass of my windshield.

The pilot shot again from his side window. This time I didn't know if I was hit.

I couldn't outrun him. I pulled back on the stick and went to full throttle climbing for a bank of stratus clouds above me. In the process, my plane slowed and the chase plane fell below, but it wouldn't take long for him to readjust.

I hoped he wasn't still shooting. I couldn't hear anything over the engine and wind noise. Finally, wisps of gray white closed in on me and I was cloaked in invisibility. Would he follow? At least he'd be flying blind if he did.

I switched on the radio and turned to Anchorage radio frequency in time to hear. "This is Cessna 8763 Foxtrot reporting a stolen Super Cub floatplane, tail number November 4677 Echo. Suspect is proceeding toward Anchorage."

While it wasn't proper protocol for pilots to announce stolen planes over the airwaves themselves, I didn't want to take any chances. I quickly changed frequencies, called Kenai Unicom and asked them to broadcast an urgent alert for anyone listening to call Vic Elmore at Kenai Flight Service. "Please ask him to meet Big Red at their old fishing spot. This is an emergency."

"Affirmative," came the response.

Using my position calculated from my entry into the clouds, I took a heading to Kenai, figuring time with light and variable winds aloft. I needed to descend over flat terrain and to avoid landing at the Kenai airport due to the stolen float plane report. Landing away from civilization, I could leave the plane and drive to Anchorage with Vic. The fellow chasing me would probably expect me to land the plane at Lake Hood, not arrive by car. I could contact the authorities and hope they would intercept him while he waited for me. Now, if I just didn't run out of fuel.

I glanced at the right visual fuel gauge tube. Not bad. When I checked the left side, I gasped. It was almost empty! A bullet must have hit the fuel line on that side.

Looking back at the tail, I could see a fine mist streaming behind me. Could I make it to Kenai losing so much fuel? It'd be close.

I switched to use only the leaking tank in order to access as much fuel as possible before it emptied.

A few minutes later, the engine sputtered as the fuel flow became inconsistent. I rechecked the gauge. Almost all fuel had drained from the right side. The left gauge remained stable. I switched to the left tank and flew on, keeping close watch as the fuel level drifted lower.

I checked the clock and the radio weather report for the cloud ceiling height at Kenai. It was time, and should be safe to descend. I let down slowly until I broke out of the clouds. The oil platforms in Cook Inlet came into view.

Wanting to avoid the Kenai control area, I dropped my altitude to 500 feet and flew outside their boundary just north of Nikiski to the designated lake.

No sign of Vic, but the fuel gauge read near empty.

I circled to land hoping bullets hadn't punctured the floats. I lined up and landed as close to shore as near the fishing spot as I could get.

The engine stuttered to a stop before I could taxi in as close as I wanted. Time for another cardio work-out. I opened the door, checked for a paddle and found one attached to the float. Standing on the front of the float, I paddled with all my strength, alternating from side-to-side, to maneuver the plane to shore. As

I pulled near, I spotted Vic's truck on the road. He had understood my message after all.

Vic parked and got out of his truck. I waved and signaled for him to catch the rope I held ready to throw so he could pull me to shore. Once he caught it and drew the plane close, I jumped into the water and waded the rest of the way in. I splashed over to where Vic stood and gave him a big hug.

"Thanks, Vic. You're my hero." I yanked the brim of his cap down in our familiar ritual.

"What's going on, Red?" Vic asked. "You're on floats now?"

"I am. Help me turn the plane around and pull her to shore so we can tie a float to that birch tree over there."

Vic rolled up his pant legs, took off his shoes, and we waded in to secure the plane. Once we finished, I untied Ken's sluice and stowed it in Vic's truck.

After Vic brushed off his feet and replaced his shoes, he turned to me, hands on his hips. "Okay now Beri, give. What's this all about?

"It's a long story. I'll fill you in on the drive." I climbed into the truck, slammed the door and turned to face him. "I have a big favor to ask…"

Chapter Thirty

"I stole the floatplane," I said, gesturing to it parked on the lake. "But only because they'd kidnapped me, and I used it to escape."

He blinked, shocked. "What?"

"Yeah, it's true."

"Wow, glad you're okay, Red."

"I'll never complain about you calling me Red again. I didn't want to use my real name on the air."

"My ears definitely perked up when I heard it, but no one else would have had a clue who sent the message."

"As soon as we're within range, I'll call an FBI agent I know and explain the situation. Then, I'll turn myself in."

"Does the FBI investigate airplane theft?" Vic asked as he started the engine and started down the gravel road toward the highway.

"Probably not unless it crosses state lines, but kidnapping is definitely in their jurisdiction."

"Good point." He gave me an evil grin. "Hope they don't arrest me for aiding and abetting a fugitive."

I poked his shoulder. "Don't worry. I'll make it clear that you only provided me a ride so I could turn myself in to the authorities. I'm anxious to get back because I found a piece of Ken's equipment at their hangar. These crooks may have captured him at some point too."

Glancing at my phone, I saw I finally had a couple of bars. I dialed Norm Underwood and explained the situation.

"I'm on my way to your office now."

"You certainly manage to get yourself into some situations," Norm said. "I'll start the wheels turning on recovering the plane. Do you have the coordinates of the lake where you left it?"

I gave them to him. "Here's the coordinates of the chop shop where they held me, too." I described where it was.

"Thanks. Good work. When do you think you'll get here?"

I glanced at Vic's speedometer. "We're on the Seward Highway now and about forty-five minutes out. And Norm? There's something I need to show you."

"I'll be waiting. I do have another situation brewing, but I should still be here."

Vic parked in the FBI parking lot. "Want me to go in with you?"

"No, but thanks. You've done enough. You might want to stay in town for a while though in case they have questions. Why don't you grab a bite and stop by my office to fill in Angie. I just need to get this straightened out. I'll call and let you know where things stand."

"It's a plan," Vic said. "Good luck in there."

I walked to the building's entrance as Vic drove away. Inside, I was greeted by a security guard. I'd forgotten about the surveillance check required before entering federal buildings. I no longer had a gun or knife on me, so figured I'd be all right.

"Please empty your pockets and place your watch, phone and any metal items on the tray before you walk through," the guard said.

I did as he requested and started through only to hear the alarm bleating. "Sorry. It must be my vest."

I started to remove my survival vest when I was surrounded by two more FBI personnel, one with their weapon drawn.

"It's just a survival vest," I said. "Maybe the fish hooks triggered the machine."

After an intense scrutiny and the removal of the vest I was allowed to pass through again, this time to blessed silence.

"Where are you going?" a female agent asked. "I'll escort you."

"May I have my belongings back first? Norm Underwood is expecting me."

"No, sorry. I'll need to hang on to them for a while, but we'll return them to

140

you later." She picked them up and handed them to the other agent who took them and walked away. "You must be mistaken about Underwood. He left the building fifteen minutes ago."

"Really, well, if that's the case, something unexpected must have come up," I said.

"I'll take you upstairs and you can explain the problem to his partner." She led me into the elevator and pushed the button for the third floor. Once we arrived, she directed me to a small conference room. "Special Agent Kelly will be with you in a few minutes."

The room held a table and four chairs and nothing else. If a camera was hidden somewhere, I couldn't spot it. After thirty minutes, I grew impatient and tried the door. Locked. *What was going on?* I hadn't taken Norm to be the type to play games with me. I debated whether to pound on the door and demand they let me out, but decided to take a nap instead. I'd just put my head down on the table when the door finally opened.

"Ms. Quinn?" A balding man with a fringe of red hair above his ears asked as he shook my hand and took a seat across from me.

"Yes, that's me." I tried to smile.

"Special Agent Underwood sends his apologies. He had to leave on a matter that couldn't wait. He didn't have time to fill me in on many details of your situation, so could you please catch me up?"

I gave him an overview, highlighting the fact I'd been held against my will and was forced to escape in my captor's float plane.

"Why didn't they restrain you?" he asked.

"They did. They tied me to a concrete tie-down, then left in a plane shortly after contacting someone by radio. My impression was they didn't expect to be gone long."

Kelly rubbed the top of his head. "Strange. You'd think one of the men would have stayed with you."

"I agree, but I took advantage by freeing myself and flying out." I showed him the cuts on my hands. "I don't think they thought I could get loose, and didn't expect I'd find a way to leave if I did."

"Why couldn't you fly your own plane? You flew in, didn't you?"

I sighed. "They'd incapacitated it by slashing the tail."

"I see. And why didn't you fly the float plane back here? Why leave it on a lake in the middle of nowhere?"

"Several reasons. One, I didn't have enough gas to reach Anchorage. Two, I knew they'd reported the plane stolen, and three, that's what they expected me to do. I didn't want them shooting at me again."

"Good thinking on your part." He stood up and turned to leave.

"And one more thing I should mention, Agent Kelly. I brought a piece of evidence you should see."

He looked down at my empty hands. "What kind of evidence?"

"I found a sluice belonging to Ken Abbott, a missing pilot. It's possible one of the parted-out planes parked outside was the rental Ken was flying. I think these guys were involved in his disappearance."

"And you think the sluice proves this?"

"Possibly, yes. I think that both the sluice and the plane—if we find it, will go a long way toward proving a connection. It could help us locate the pilot."

"I see why you thought it was important. Where is this sluice now?"

"I brought it with me. It's in my friend's truck. He's waiting for me at my office."

"You realize the sluice lost its value as evidence the moment you removed it from the scene. You should have left it where it was."

I cringed. "Sorry, I didn't think of that. I was afraid it would be taken from the hangar, if I left it there."

Kelly stood and went for the door. "I'll be back after I get it."

"Wait. I'll go with you."

"You need to stay here until we get this stolen plane issue cleared up."

"No. I can't just sit here. My father is in the hospital. I need to check on him. My dog needs to be fed. I have things to do."

"Sorry, Ms. Quinn. I'm waiting to hear from the crew Underwood sent to the GPS locations you gave him. Until we clear up the stolen plane report, I have to detain you."

I sighed in resignation. "Can I at least have my phone so I can check in with my family and my office?"

"Can't help you there until we finish with it. We're waiting on a warrant now. However, I can let you make a call from our landline. I'll make that happen before I leave."

Several phone calls and a long nap later, I raised my head from the table to see Norm Underwood facing me on the other side.

"I'm so glad to see you," I said. "This has turned into quite the ordeal."

"Sorry I had to leave before you arrived, but it wouldn't have changed anything if I'd been here. These things take time."

"I get it. So where do we stand now?"

"Your story checks out. Your plane was still parked where you said you left it. We've recovered the float plane and Agent Kelly picked up the sluice. The chop shop was locked and deserted when we got there. We're waiting for warrants to get inside."

I stood and stretched. "Good. Please let me know if you identify the owners of the planes parked outside the chop shop. One of them may be the one my student was flying when he went missing."

"Will do."

"So, I can leave now?"

"Yes. You can pick up your phone and belongings from the clerk on your way out. Thanks for your help." He shook my hand and smiled. "I expect you've single-handedly opened at least three new lines of investigation for us to pursue. We'll be in touch."

I high-tailed it out of there. I didn't want them to find another reason to detain me.

Chapter Thirty-one

Dad's condition remained the same. He'd been moved from intensive care to a neurology floor. His color was no longer dusky, and his bruises were beginning to fade, but he remained comatose. The nursing station contacted his doctor so he could give me an update.

"Overall, more stable, no change in mental status."

I'd figured that out for myself. Still, I thanked the doctor and said I appreciated them taking such good care of Dad. I stayed with Dad for a few minutes holding his hand, talking to him, but I didn't mention anything about my recent excursion.

I left and stopped at the office. Vic sat patiently at my desk regaling Angie with stories of his fishing exploits.

"Beri," Angie said. "So glad you're safe, but I hear we have another plane out of commission."

"Just some damage to the fabric of the tail. Dean should be able to get her ship-shape in no time. Not sure when the authorities will release her though."

Angie grabbed a note from her desk. "I have one bit of bad news for you. Your security company called. Apparently, the camera was destroyed before it could record the attack on your dad. How's he doing anyway?"

My voice quavered as my emotions from the entire day sank in. "He's making a little progress."

Vic stood and moved away from my desk. "A Feeb came by and confiscated your sluice. Asked me a few questions and left about an hour ago."

I gave him a bear hug. "Thanks for everything, Vic. You're a true friend. If I can ever reciprocate, let me know."

"No problem, Red. Always available for a damsel in distress. Especially one who taught me how to gut a fish." He walked to the door. "I'd better get going. Got an early shift tomorrow."

"Give me a call next time you're in town. I'll grill you a steak to go with the beer I already owe you."

"You're on. Nice to rack up some points."

Tiger jumped up and greeted me with paws on my shoulder and kisses to my face. He seemed none the worse for my absence. I checked the water pail in his run and found it full to the top with a dish of dry food sitting beside it.

"Somebody's been watching out for you, boy. Ross, I'll bet," I said and picked up the kibble bowl. "Let's take this inside. Don't want to attract bears to compete with you out here."

We went in through the garage, shut the door and entered the kitchen. Everything appeared just as I'd left it early that morning. I walked through the rest of the house before taking a quick shower and changing to fresh clothes.

Feeling better, I poured a glass of wine and sank down into Dad's recliner. I rubbed my wrists, still raw from dragging the tie-down and sighed. I was lucky to be here.

Tiger rested his chin on my knee and gazed soulfully into my eyes. "It's too quiet around here isn't it, boy?"

I picked up my phone and dialed. Ross answered on the first ring.

"Beri. Heard you were back."

"Yes. It feels good. Thanks for watching out for Tiger. I was lucky to return as soon as I did."

"No problem. Angie was worried, and I didn't want my buddy to starve if you were delayed."

"Sounds like I need to get you a key to the house."

"Now, that sounds like an idea. Do I have to wait for you to go out of town to use it?"

I laughed. "No, any time. Speaking of which, I could use some company now. Why don't you come over?"

Ross poured me a second glass of Merlot, and I moved over to the sofa to sit next to him.

"This feels nice." I rested my head on his shoulder. "I've been wound too tight lately."

"Mmmhmm," Ross sighed. "Glad to help." His hand massaged my neck and moved down my shoulder to my arm. When he noticed my wrist, he picked up my hand and kissed it. "All better?"

"Definitely."

His lips moved to mine.

As our kiss grew in intensity, I started to pull away.

Ross held me closer. "What are you afraid of? I'd never do anything to hurt you."

"I know that."

He grinned. "Then let's try that again."

We did.

I hadn't intended to fall in love. It would complicate my life even more than it already was, but somehow, I didn't care. I kept kissing him.

Chapter Thirty-two

The next morning after swinging by the hospital to check on Dad, I walked into the office and sat down at my desk.

Angie greeted me with a cheery "Good morning. Norm Underwood called." She handed me a slip of paper. "He said he wanted to give you an update on the status of your report. I took the liberty of scheduling an appointment for you to meet with him later this morning. Give him a call if you need to change it."

I gave her a sideways glance. "No, it's fine. Thanks."

Thinking I'd tie up some loose ends in the meantime, I checked online for Nico's phone number. I wanted to try contacting him one last time. The number listed was the same number Paige had already been trying, and sure enough, I had the same result. No answer and full mailbox. E-mail hadn't worked, phoning hadn't, either. Resorting to snail mail, I typed a quick note asking him to contact me, sealed it in an envelope and addressed it to the home address his landlord had given me.

Next, I found the phone number for FSDO, called and asked for Don. This time I had better luck.

"Hello, what can I do for you, Beri?"

"Hi Don. Sorry to bother you again, but I wanted to ask one more question."

"Sure. Hope I know the answer. What's the question?"

"Finding out Ken's second flight plan was generated by someone other than

Ken may be an important clue in figuring out what really happened to him. Is there any way to track the source of that call?"

"Not really. It was a radio transmission, not a phone call or it'd be easier to trace. We routinely assume the airplane tail number the pilot gives us is accurate. We don't verify it in any way. If it came from an airliner, we could check it against radar, but for a Super Cub I don't know of any way to get that information."

Not giving up, I asked, "Are you aware of any instances when something like this happened before?"

"Nope. Never heard of it."

"Okay, thanks for your help." I hung up the phone. Another dead end. This was frustrating. How could I prove who'd called in the flight plan and why they did?

It was almost time for my appointment with Norm. I gathered my things, surveyed the contents of my purse to make sure I wouldn't run into any problems getting past FBI security, and left.

As I drove past Hanratty's, I noticed a white SUV parked behind the building. I told myself it was unlikely to be the one I saw the night Buzz was shot. There are lots of white SUVs in town, but it might be worth checking out. On an impulse, I turned and drove to the back of the lot. Sure enough, I spotted an orange decal pasted in the lower left corner of the rear windshield.

I tried to call Norm on my cell phone to see if he could meet me at Hanratty's, but the call went to voice mail. Figuring I'd report it when I saw him, I jotted down the license plate number, left, and drove to the FBI building.

Norm rose when I entered his office and shook my hand. "Beri. Thanks for coming in."

"Angie says you have new information for me."

"That I do. We've confirmed the planes parked outside the site you found were stolen. After we got a search warrant, we confirmed the plane parked inside was stolen, too. That plane was brand spanking new and hadn't been scavenged like most of the others. Your plane had only minor damage to the tail. The plane Ken Abbott rented was reduced to an empty shell. You definitely uncovered a chop-shop operation. We're still trying to determine the ownership of the rest of the planes and of the building. It's listed under an obscure corporation."

"Have you notified Kaitlin that you found her plane?"

"Yes. To say she was pleased would be a definite understatement."

"When can I pick up mine? I'd like to fly Dean out to repair the tail so I can put it to use. We're running short on planes at the moment."

"We've confiscated the float plane you took, but you can recover yours any time. It would be a good idea, however, to coordinate with us so we can provide back-up in case you encounter any problems."

"I'll check with Dean and contact you later today."

"About another matter…" Norm paused and gave me a sheepish look. "I think I may have misled you."

"How's that?" I cocked my head to one side.

"I've spent some time thoroughly reviewing Alex Veronin's background and business dealings. I was confident I'd find shady partners and criminal activity."

"And did you?"

"Not really. True, there have been rumors of mob connections, but nothing I was able to confirm. And it turns out you're not the only mapping business Cartos wants to acquire. Veronin's been putting out feelers in four or five western states. Word's out he wants to expand, become the major provider this side of the Mississippi and eventually go public with the business." Norm stood and paced back and forth behind the table. "I still wasn't satisfied, so I checked to see if any of these other businesses had experienced problems with threats or sabotage like you. It turns out they haven't. Most of them seemed to feel they'd been treated fairly. Some even said more than fairly."

I swallowed. "No threats?"

"Apparently not. I think his comment sounded like a threat because I'd set the stage for you to think he had mob connections. Now, I can't be sure that's true. If, however, it turns out he's behind the organization that owns the chop shop, I could change my thinking still again."

"Hmmm. I may have one more thing for you," I said. "On my way over, I noticed a car matching the description of the SUV I saw speeding away the night Buzz was killed at our hangar. It even had a decal like the one I remember seeing in the rear window."

"Sounds like a police matter. Have you contacted them?"

"Not yet, but I did get the license plate number."

"Why don't you give it to me, and I'll run it. It's hard to know at this point what's connected to our case and what's not. I'll be in touch with the police, too."

I left, befuddled. Everything I'd believed to be true was now in doubt, but what else would explain the bizarre events of the last few weeks?

Chapter Thirty-three

The police seemed singularly unimpressed by my report of the SUV I'd spotted, but I couldn't get it out of my mind. When I left work for the day, I noted it was no longer parked behind Hanratty's building. I decided to stop and check on the pending part order I was still waiting for from him. While there, I could ask Ace about who the vehicle belonged to. Surely, he'd talk to me this time.

A bell jangled when I opened the front door of the store. The lights were on, but no one appeared behind the counter. I waited a few minutes without seeing anyone. "Hello," I called out. "Can I get some help please?"

No one answered.

"Ace, are you in the storeroom?" I called out in a loud voice.

Still no answer. I stood, shifting my weight from one foot to the other for a few minutes. Impatient, I reached behind the counter gate, unlatched it and went through. The door to the stock room stood open so I walked inside, calling for Ace.

The light was dimmer here, and I didn't hear a sound. This was starting to feel eerie. He wouldn't have gone home and left the front door unlocked. That wasn't like him. Besides, the car I assumed was his was still parked outside.

I started to think I should leave. When I pulled out my phone to try calling Ace's home number, I tripped and fell to my knees. My phone clattered to the cement floor. I checked to see what caused me to fall and spotted a piece of chrome-moly-steel tubing projecting out into the aisle from under a work table that stood against the wall. My eyes tracked the length of tubing to the hand that grasped it. It belonged to the body of Ace Hanratty stuffed beneath the work table.

I fought the scream that rose to my throat and reached underneath to check his wrist for a pulse. There was none. I picked up my phone, hoping it still worked. Despite a small crack in the screen, my 9-1-1 call went through.

The total silence in the room increased my sense of unease. With only Ace's car left in the parking lot, I felt fairly certain the murderer was gone.

I searched the area while waiting for the police to arrive. While I didn't want to disturb the crime scene, I wanted to take a close look at the body so I picked up a flashlight sitting on the table with the hem of my shirt. After clicking it on, I directed the beam of light into the darkness beneath the table.

Immediately, I spotted the bullet hole in Ace's chest and the puddle of blood pooling out from his body.

Carefully, I returned the flashlight to its original position beside a bottle of laundry bluing and a rack of test tubes. I wondered what Ace did with them. I didn't see a washing machine in the vicinity. As nothing else seemed unusual or out of place, I decided to follow the police dispatcher's advice and return to my car to wait for the police.

While I waited, I tried calling Norm to see if he'd had any luck identifying the owner of the SUV. Once again, the call went to voice mail. This time I left a message letting him know what I'd discovered.

A stream of police cars screamed into the parking lot, lights flashing. I opened my car door and got out.

One of the same officers who'd responded to the drive-by shooting spotted me and frowned.

"You again," he said. "What is it with you and shootings?"

"I don't know, but whatever it is I'm ready for it to come to an end."

I related the sequence of events beginning with the SUV that had caught my attention and led to my finding the body.

"Excuse me, ma'am?" another officer interrupted. "Did you say you knew the identity of the victim?"

"Yes, as I told the dispatcher, he's the owner of the business. Ace Hanratty."

"Got it. We need you to wait here in the cruiser while we secure the crime scene. If you think of anything else, let us know."

Almost an hour later, the same officer walked up to me. "Let me introduce Detective Diaz," he said. "He'll take the lead on the case."

The detective, boyish in appearance except for the deep furrows between his eyes, pulled out a pen and note pad. "Tell me what happened. Start from the beginning."

"I've told the other officers everything I know."

"I'm sure you have, but we have to be thorough. Did you touch anything while you were inside?"

"Yes. I probably touched the counter, I rang the bell, opened the latch to go to the back. Once inside, I fell over a rod and dropped my phone. I may have touched the rod, and my hands touched the floor."

"Okay, that will do it for now. We'll need to tape your statement at the station. Come with me and I'll drive you downtown."

I knew I'd never see the parts Dean needed now, but it didn't matter. Ace had been a disgruntled old man, but he hadn't deserved to die that way.

Chapter Thirty-four

The next morning, I sat in the recording room following an interminable rehash of the events of the afternoon before. Detective Diaz stood and led me out to his desk. It resided in a two-sided cubicle in a large room lined with two rows of identical units. The almost empty surface held only a computer terminal and a pad of paper.

Diaz pulled out a chair beside the desk for me and folded his lanky frame to sit in front of his computer. An inebriated man's rantings in a nearby cubicle and a couple of officers at a corner desk chatting about a golf tournament provided background noise.

Diaz seemed oblivious to the distractions. "Let's take a minute to go over a few details," he said.

"I don't have anything to add to what I've told you."

Diaz checked his notes. "You told us you stopped to ask the victim about an SUV you'd noticed parked outside his building earlier that afternoon. I'm wondering why you waited. Why didn't you stop to talk to him at the time you saw the SUV?"

"Because I had an appointment with the FBI. I didn't have time. I mentioned what I'd noticed to Agent Underwood and gave him the number of the license plate."

Diaz's brows wrinkled. "Why did you do that?"

"He's involved with the troopers investigating a kidnapping and plane theft incident I reported recently. I didn't really expect there was a connection to the SUV, but I thought I should inform him just in case."

"I see. And after you stopped at Hanratty's business, why did you decide to go into the storeroom?"

"Mr. Hanratty and my father are cousins. They've done business together for many years. I've continued the tradition since I took over the company. In addition to asking about the SUV, I planned to ask about a part he had on back order for one of my airplanes. It was so unlike him to leave his register unattended when the front door was unlocked, I thought something might be wrong."

Diaz rubbed his chin and gave me a searching look. "And did you touch anything when you went exploring?"

"Only what I told you last night."

"Nothing else?"

"Well, I suppose when I left to wait in the car, I touched the front door to get out."

"Didn't you tell us you used a flashlight to better see the body?"

"I did, but I didn't touch it directly. I picked it up using my shirttail."

"Very astute of you."

"Unfortunately, I've had reason to be more aware of crime procedures lately."

Diaz nodded his head. "I'll say. Any idea why someone would want to kill Mr. Hanratty?"

"None. He could be prickly at times, but nothing that I could imagine inciting violence."

"I've been in contact with Agent Underwood about the kidnapping incident. Any connection with Mr. Hanratty to that case?"

"Like I said before, I can't think of any."

"How about the assault on your father or the incidents at your place of business?" he asked.

"I've wondered about the attack on Dad, but I don't have any proof of a connection. Since Dad is still in a coma, I can't ask him."

"Exactly *what* made you wonder about Hanratty?"

"I recently came across some old letters that indicated he harbored a grudge about some gold claims my dad and he inherited years ago while they were in the military."

"Can I get copies of those letters?"

"Sure, I don't see why not, but I can't imagine why Hanratty would attack Dad all these years later. That doesn't make sense. Why would he wait so long?"

"Who knows, but we'll check it out as a possibility." He stood and pushed his chair back. "Okay then, that's all for now. We'll need to get your fingerprints for exclusionary purposes. When you finish, I'll have paperwork ready for you to sign."

"Before you go, I'd like to ask you a question, Detective Diaz."

"Let's hear it."

I turned to him. "What did your trace on the license plate of the SUV turn up?"

"I can't comment on that right now. We're still investigating."

I didn't let him see my expression as he left.

Fingerprinted and statement completed, I asked Diaz for a copy of my statement. He seemed surprised, but made me one. I took it and walked out of police headquarters.

"When were you going to tell me?" a familiar voice asked.

I whirled to find Ross standing beside a parked car. "Careful, you're going to set off that car alarm if you get any closer."

"Not to worry. I don't think it has one," Ross said. "Now, stop dodging my question."

"I'm not dodging it. So much happened so quickly, I haven't had a chance to talk to anybody. By the time the police released me last night, I figured you'd be sleeping after you returned from the cross-country you had scheduled."

"Uh huh. And what about this morning?"

"I've been here all morning finishing my statement."

Ross took my arm and steered me toward his Jeep parked at the far end of the parking lot. "Sorry. You've been through a lot. Let's find someplace else to talk."

He drove to the Park Strip on Ninth Avenue and parked near a decommissioned Alaska Railroad steam-engine. We watched a small boy climbing on the snow plow while his smiling mother kept watch.

"Okay, give," he said. "Tell me what happened."

"I've gone over it so many times with the police, why don't you just read my copy of the statement I signed. When you finish, I'll answer any questions you have."

"If that's the way you want to do it, I'm game."

While Ross read, I watched the mother lift her son up to pretend he was engineer of the train. I used to do the same thing with Jack when he was younger. It made me miss him all the more.

Ross finished reading and peered up at me. "Why didn't you call me so I could go with you to Hanratty's?"

"Why would I? I didn't expect any trouble. I just wanted to ask about the plane part and the SUV. I wasn't even sure it was the one I'd seen outside our hangar."

"Honey, you could have walked in on the murder in progress."

"I suppose I could have, but I didn't." I met his eyes. "Don't you think you're being over-protective?"

"Maybe, but after all that's happened…"

I interrupted. "No, you are."

"Under normal circumstances, maybe. But you have to admit you've been a magnet for trouble lately."

"I appreciate your concern, I do. I'm grateful for all your help when I've needed it, but you worry too much."

"I don't think so." Ross smiled and gave my hand a squeeze. "But I'll stop hovering if you'll promise to call me—if you do sense danger."

"Will do. I already have a good track record for doing just that."

My cell phone rang and I pulled it out of my pocket and answered.

"Beri? Beri Quinn?"

"Yes. This is Beri."

"This is Sandra Beck. I'm an RN at Providence Hospital. You asked to be notified of any changes in your father's condition. I thought you'd want to know that he's awake."

"He's awake? That's wonderful! Thank you. I'll be right there." I hung up the phone and my eyes started to water. "Ross, let's go see Dad."

Chapter Thirty-five

Once Ross and I entered Dad's room, we realized everything had changed. While the room itself was the same, the atmosphere felt completely different. No longer did technology rule the senses. Now, all I could see was Dad's smile. It dominated everything else and melted my heart.

"Dad?" I rushed to hug him. "I'm so glad you're feeling better."

"Cupcake." His voice was low and slower than usual, but it was so good to hear.

He was propped up by pillows, and he held a cup of apple juice in his right hand. "Thought I was going to spill this the way you squeezed me."

"I was so worried."

"Huh. You should know I'm tough." He set the juice down on the bedside table. "How's Jack?"

"Having a good time, I hope. He left for Germany last night."

"He's a fine boy."

"Yes." I squeezed his hand. "Dad, do you remember anything about what happened?"

His smile dimmed. "I'd rather not talk about it."

"Sure, that's okay. There's time for that later. Right now, we're just happy you're awake."

His eyelids drifted downward. "I think I need to nap a little while, sweetheart."
He turned to Ross. "Take care of her for me, son."

"I sure will, Frank. Get some rest now."

After a long nap, I visited with Dad again briefly before he shooed me out.
He seemed more himself, more alert than earlier, but he clearly didn't want to
answer questions.

"Sweetheart, don't get me wrong. I love spending time with you, but I don't
want you to feel you have to be here every moment. You have responsibilities
and work to do."

"But Dad, I *want* to be here with you."

"That makes me happy, but I'd be happier if I didn't feel I was such a nuisance.
Doc says he's moving me to rehab later today, so you go on. Get some work
done. Do something productive."

I laughed. "I get it, I get it. You don't want me around. I'll check on you
tomorrow. Love you, Dad." I left by way of the elevator and smiled all the way
to the ground floor. Dad was back to his old self.

Chapter Thirty-six

Dean hunched over his work bench. He appeared to be inspecting the seal on an oil pump. His hands glistened with oil. I broke his concentration when I walked up beside him.

"Beri. What can I do for you?"

"I do have something, but first I wanted to ask if you'd heard about Ace Hanratty's death?"

"Sure have, but don't know any details. Just what was on the news this morning."

"I don't know a lot, either. He was shot. It happened late in the afternoon. I left work and stopped to check on the part we'd ordered and instead found his body."

"No one deserves that. Not even Hanratty."

"True." I sat on a stool next to the work bench. "I also wanted to ask you about repairing the tail on the Cub I flew out to the chop shop. The FBI says it can be released, but they want you to coordinate the trip out to repair it with them as a safety precaution."

Dean wiped his oil-covered hands and pulled out his calendar. "I can go whenever you're free. Is it mainly fabric damage?"

"That was my impression."

"The tear shouldn't take too long to repair. I'll get the supplies together and be ready when you set it up."

"Thank you. I'll ask Ross to fly us out. Will we be able to fly back in the Cub the same day you make the repairs?"

"We should. Unless we run into problems we don't know about yet."

His statement had me biting my lip. The way things were going, I guessed I should expect the unexpected.

I left for my appointment with aviation attorney, Gerald Sullivan, anxious to hear if he'd succeeded in staving off my license suspension. With several small photography projects pending and students to teach, I couldn't afford to be grounded.

Sullivan's office, located near the courthouse in what passed for an Anchorage high-rise, was on the fifth floor with a view of Cook Inlet. I took the elevator and walked in the door just as a brass clock behind the receptionist's desk chimed a soft triple note marking the hour.

"Right on time," the receptionist said and gave me a big smile. She led me down a short hall and through a heavy office door.

Gerald sat behind a large ebony desk positioned in front of a wall of glass overlooking the water. If it had been my office, I'd have been facing the other way, but maybe he wanted his clients to appreciate the view.

"Hello, Beri." He stood and shook my hand. "Please take a seat. Have you heard anything from the FAA since we last spoke?"

I sat in one of the gray, leather and chrome chairs in front of his desk. "No. Everything's the same as far as I know."

"Interesting." He opened a file folder and extracted a sheet of paper. "In that case, I'll report on my conversation with the NTSB. I spoke to a chief investigator I've done business with before. He agreed with me that the FAA action against you is highly irregular. I asked him to review your mechanic's finding regarding intentional fuel contamination. He assured me he would. I also notified Ms. Hermann with the FAA that we were appealing the order to suspend your license, and asked for a hearing at the earliest opportunity. She gave me a date that was months in the future. I made a phone call to Washington this morning, stating this was unacceptable. My contact assured me that the suspension would be put on hold until after the hearing and local staff would be encouraged to reconsider the delay in scheduling."

"Thank you! That is such a relief." I exhaled the breath I'd been holding. "I was afraid I wouldn't be able to fly after next week."

"That's why I get the big bucks," he said, only half in jest. "I'm mystified why you've had such problems with the agency. They're usually more reasonable, but someone in this office clearly doesn't like you."

"I'm sure of it, but I don't know why."

He stood and walked around his desk to hand me a copy of a letter confirming the changes in scheduling my suspension. "You should receive a formal confirmation from the FAA in the next few days."

"Thanks again, Mr. Sullivan. You can't know how much this means to me."

"Call me Sully, please. And thank Gracie for sending you to see me. We went to law school together. She's quite a gal."

"That she is," I agreed.

"One more thing," Sully said, "please advise your mechanic to expect to hear from the NTSB inspector."

I returned to the office feeling like a huge boulder had been removed from me. The problem wasn't solved, but at least I could fly for the foreseeable future. We could keep the business operating.

Angie greeted me with a broad smile, waving a slip of paper in the air.

"What?" I asked.

"Paige came by. Sorry you missed her, but she brought a check! She paid her bill. Our bank account rejoices."

"My, this is a good day. Did she say anything?"

"Just that she's excited about your new lead on Ken's flight plan. She'll check in with you later. She has to go out of town again and wanted to drop the check off before she left."

"I have more good news. My attorney managed to get my pilot's license suspension put on hold."

"Wonderful!" Angie high-fived me, her wide smile lighting her face. "Oh, and there's this…" She picked up a slip of paper from her desk and handed it to me. "I almost forgot. It's a message to call Norm Underwood. He said he expects to be in the office all afternoon."

"Thanks, I'll call him now."

Norm answered on the first ring. "Beri. I hear you've been stirring up trouble again."

"Not me. Trouble finds me without any stirring. Sounds like you've heard about Ace Hanratty's murder."

"Yes, sorry I didn't get the message you left as things unfolded, although I doubt I'd have given as much significance to the SUV as you did."

"No problem. Have you heard whether the police have made any progress in their investigation? I met with them earlier today, but they didn't share any news with me. For all I know, I may be their chief suspect."

Norm snorted. "I doubt that, but it's their case so I'm the wrong person to ask."

"Does that mean you don't have any info, *or* you aren't willing to share what you have?"

"Nothing I can talk about for now, but I appreciate your trying to contact me with your observations. I hope you'll continue to do that."

"I'll try, but honestly, it's hard for me to know how everything that's happened fits together—what's important to you and what is the purview of the police."

"I understand the problem. It's always difficult to sort out jurisdiction, especially when we law enforcement agencies don't always work together as well as we should."

"I'll leave it to you. Tell me if I'm out of line when I call you."

"Sure. Keep me informed. I'll sort it out."

I hung up and sat wondering what the FBI would uncover about the ownership of the chop shop and whether we'd ever find a relationship to what had happened to Ken.

Chapter Thirty-seven

After a quick trip home, I returned to the hospital to find Dad snoozing in his wheelchair.

"Dad. Wake up. I need to talk to you." I tapped his arm gently.

"What?" He yawned and opened his eyes. "Sorry. I must have dozed off waiting to go to physical therapy."

"I'll hurry, because it sounds like PT will be here soon. I have some important questions to ask."

He raised his eyebrows. "Okay, I'm listening."

I dropped the packet of letters from his closet into his lap. "I didn't intend to snoop, but I looked through your file box when I needed to find your insurance information for the hospital. I found these. Why didn't you tell me about Ace feeling cheated out of his inheritance?"

"It's better not to dwell on sensitive family matters. It can only make things worse."

I sat down across from him on the bed. "So did Ace have a legitimate complaint against you?"

He took a deep breath. "His complaint was valid, but I wasn't the cause of the trouble. I was in Vietnam when it happened. His mother kept him in the dark because she wanted him to stay home after he was discharged from the army.

As she put it, she didn't want him galivanting off to Alaska on a stupid treasure hunt. She realized he'd want to go work the claims if he knew about them. By the time Ace found out, too much time had passed. The Alaska Native Claims Settlement Act was in force. Ace never forgave his mother, and he also blamed me because I managed to keep my claims."

"It seems unreasonable to blame you."

"I agree, but he was overly emotional about it. I think it clouded his thinking, and he's grown more bitter over the years. It's why I tried to support his business for so long. It wasn't much, but it was all I could think to do."

"Okay. I'm starting to understand—was it Ace who attacked you?"

"I don't want to press charges. It's water under the bridge."

"Dad, he was murdered."

Dad jerked to attention. "What? Ace murdered? Who killed him?"

"I don't know. He was shot in his stockroom. That's one reason I needed to know the whole story so I can piece things together."

"The police stopped by to ask questions. I told them I couldn't remember because I didn't want to make things worse for him, but it was Ace who beat me. He wanted the gold he thought I'd brought back from visiting my claim."

"You didn't have it though, did you? You gave it to me to put in the office safe."

"The nuggets, yes. The rest I'd already deposited in the bank. Ace didn't believe me. He almost seemed deranged."

"I'd say deranged is a generous description of his behavior. He almost killed you."

I called Detective Diaz to give him Dad's information.

"Thanks, Ms. Quinn. I'll send someone over to take his statement. I'm glad his memory finally returned. What you say fits nicely with the evidence we've uncovered."

"Really. How did you figure it out?"

"We found your dad's wallet and a few of his belongings in a locked metal cashbox at the crime scene."

"Hmm. I wondered if it could be related to the trace on the license plate?"

"No. Nothing like that."

"So who did the SUV belong to?"

"I'd rather not say right now. We're still investigating how it might relate to Hanratty's murder. If it relates at all."

As I hung up, I couldn't help but wonder what else the detective was keeping from me, and why he was so secretive about the SUV.

Chapter Thirty-eight

I sat up in bed in the middle of the night, struck by unanswered questions jumbled together with my dreams. What evidence had the police collected from the murder scene? I knew Diaz hadn't told me everything. Could any of it provide a clue to help me find Ken? Why hadn't I thought to ask Diaz?

Sleep no longer on my agenda, I carefully got out of bed so I wouldn't wake Ross, grabbed a notepad and started listing my primary questions:

> *Was anything found linking Ace to Ken?*
> *What was in the locked box with Dad's wallet?*
> *What did they find on Ace's computer?*
> *Did the FAA find any counterfeit parts in Ace's inventory?*

Diaz hadn't been forthcoming about the license plate, but perhaps if they knew something that would help find a missing pilot, they'd be more cooperative. It was frustrating to be an outsider to the investigation. I understood why the police didn't like to reveal their findings, but I needed more information *now*. I couldn't wait until they closed their case.

It was far too early to contact Diaz. He wasn't likely to be cooperative if I woke him in the wee hours of the morning. I dressed, left a quick note for Ross and headed to the office. I decided I would prepare for a pending flying job now and talk to Diaz after I finished the job. I checked the weather, loaded the infra-red film I needed to photograph a sampling of trees damaged by birch bark beetles for the Chugach National Park Service. The area was nearby and the six flight lines required wouldn't take long to finish. I did find them challenging, however, due to the rough terrain in the area. It was difficult to navigate the elevation changes and stay on line. The effort kept me on my toes, but as I expected, the project took less than an hour to complete.

After dropping the exposed IR film off at the office, I picked up a box of pastries from the Flying Dutchman Bakery and started for police headquarters. With any luck, I could catch Detective Diaz in a talkative mood.

The officer at the desk directed me to take a seat while he called Diaz. He seemed surprised when the detective agreed to talk to me.

A few minutes later, Diaz appeared, shook my hand and led me past several cubicles, including one where an officer consoled a weeping woman. When we reached his desk, Diaz pulled over a chair for me.

"What gives?" he asked.

I handed him the box of goodies. "These are to soften you up because I really need some answers. I hope you like chocolate.

"I woke up last night, and realized everything started when my student pilot disappeared. There must be some connection to the crimes that followed. I can't think of any other reason I would be at the center of such a cascade of disasters. If I had more answers, maybe I could finally find my missing student."

"This is all news to me. What student?"

"Ken Abbott. You may have heard about it. He went missing July 18. He was flying a Super Cub. Someone filed a phony flight plan which misdirected the CAP search team. He hasn't been found, and the search has been discontinued."

"And you think this is connected to the Hanratty murder—how?"

"That's what I'm trying to figure out, but it's hard to do when I don't have any information." I recounted the series of events including Buzz's murder, my sabotaged plane, the attack on Dad and my kidnapping. "It can't all be coincidence."

"When you rattle it all off like that I can see your point. I don't see a connection though."

"I can't either, although the SUV may indicate the two murders are related. You could help me by answering some questions."

"Me first. What's this about a sabotaged plane? I haven't heard anything about it. And I don't know much about the kidnapping, either."

"I was held against my will at a remote aviation chop shop. Eventually, I escaped in the kidnapper's plane. The FBI and the troopers handled it, and since I got away on my own there wasn't much about it in the press. The sabotaged plane and my subsequent crash landing has been handled by the

FAA. Everything's been so disjointed with different agencies involved that I think something important could easily have been missed."

Diaz steepled his hands against his chin and rocked in his chair. "It's highly unorthodox in an open investigation to share information with a civilian, but give me a list of your questions and I'll run them by the Sergeant. We'll see what we can do."

I handed him the list I'd torn from my notebook.

He scanned it briefly. "Hmm, maybe. Don't know anything about counterfeit parts, and the computer download is especially unlikely."

"But it probably has the most potential to help."

"Wait here. I'll see if I can catch the Sergeant."

While he was gone, I listened to the neighboring woman's weeping escalate into wailing. Whatever had happened in her case couldn't be good. An officer escorted an older gentleman into a cubicle against the wall. I realized Detective Diaz was generous to take so much time with me in this busy place.

Diaz returned to his chair and handed me several sheets of paper. "Sarge agreed we should do what we can to assist in finding your lost pilot. This is a print-out of the evidence we collected and copies of any printed material we have. Everything's been logged into the evidence room so I won't physically show it to you. We do ask, however, that you use discretion. We don't want to hear about any of this on the news."

"Thank you. I appreciate this more than you know."

"If anything jumps out at you that might help in this investigation, give me a call."

"Of course."

He rose, indicating our time was over, and patted the bakery box. "Thanks for breakfast. I was sick of my diet anyway."

Chapter Thirty-nine

The hands on the kitchen clock approached midnight as Ross and I finished reviewing the evidence report from the crime scene of Ace Hanratty's murder. Ross threw his hands up in the air. "Interesting, but I don't see anything that will help. Do you?"

I rubbed my eyes. Tiredness was starting to set in. "Yes, I think I do. The cash box is a treasure trove."

"How so? Aside from the six hundred dollars in bills?" He scratched his head. "I'm sure your dad will appreciate getting his wallet and watch back. They definitely identify Ace as your dad's attacker, but we already knew that."

I picked up a copy of a small pamphlet and a computer-generated print-out of a map with a location circled in red. "This is what I find fascinating. What do you see here?"

Ross studied the page. His face brightened. "This must be Ken's real destination the day he disappeared."

"Right. I think it's the location of Ken's gold claim. And this instruction pamphlet explains how Ace found it. It describes how to operate a GPS tracker."

"So you think he attached it to Ken's plane and followed him?"

"I do. Ken's plane would likely fly below 12,000 feet so the tracker should work. Even if he couldn't follow in real time, it would reveal his ultimate destination."

"So would his Emergency Locator Beacon."

I raised my eyebrows and shrugged. "If it were activated, but it wouldn't be, after an uneventful flight. Ace was obsessed with the gold claims he thought he should have inherited. I think he may have seen Ken's nugget interview on television and decided to find his secret location."

"And filed the erroneous flight plan to distract searchers?"

"It sounds far-fetched, but I think he saw it as an opportunity to steal Ken's claim. After attacking Ken, he must have left and picked up an accomplice to fly him back to take Ken's plane. He left Ken helpless and assumed he wouldn't survive."

"An evil man," Ross said. "But why would someone kill Ace? Ken might have motive, but he wouldn't have opportunity."

"His accomplice?" I thought for a moment. "There has to be more to the story. Perhaps the inventory spreadsheet the police found will help give us some answers. But now that we think we know Ken's last location, we can try to find him. I'm going to catch a few winks and leave in the morning."

"Count me in," Ross said. "You're not going without me."

We loaded ourselves and our gear into my Cessna 180. It was slower than the twin, but we'd have more landing options with the smaller plane.

I hadn't flown with Ross before. It felt good. We'd have to plan a trip together sometime soon. We could cover a lot of territory alternating piloting and sleeping, although it would be more fun to keep each other company and enjoy the scenery together. After flying a little over an hour, Alice Creek came into view. My heart pounded in anticipation. *Could this be the day we'd find Ken?*

"Okay, we're approaching the location now," I said. "I hope if Ken's down there, he'll be out in the open. It would make sense for him to want to stay close to the water, so I'll try following the stream to the river. He might have thought he'd have better odds of being found there."

I flew down the center of the creek at an altitude of 700 feet. Ross scanned one side of the creek while I searched the other. We spotted two bears hunting for salmon in the water, and a few spawned-out humpies on the far bank, but no Ken.

"How far is it to the river?" Ross asked. "It's hard to see anything through all the brush."

"It's about thirty more miles. We'll keep searching. It appears like the brush thins out a bit up ahead."

"Wait, what's that?"

I stared in the direction Ross pointed. A distress signal made of dead wood and rocks stood in contrast to a short stretch of gravel-covered beach.

"You can land there, can't you?"

"Sure. That's probably why Ken chose this spot for his signal. There aren't many clearings to choose from."

Sunlight glared off the few ripples on the surface of the water. Since wind wasn't a problem, I made several passes and touched down, glad to feel firm ground under the tires. At least I wouldn't have to deal with mud slowing me down during take-off when we departed.

We climbed out of the plane and surveyed the area. No sign of Ken or anyone else. No sound except the occasional whir of a mosquito. "Let's climb up the bank. Ken would be weak by now, and he'd probably want to keep some distance from the bears' fishing ground."

Ross pushed through the thick stand of alders to make his way up the bank.

"Hey, turn to your left," I said. "The brush is broken. It may be a trail."

"Let's hope Ken blazed it and not a bear," Ross said.

"No kidding. I brought my gun, in case, but I sure don't want to have to use it."

After trekking for a while, I paused to catch my breath. "Shhh. I think I heard something."

It was weak but unmistakable. A human voice, but I couldn't make out any words.

"Hello. Anybody there?" I turned toward the sound of the voice that answered, and this time a glint of silver caught my eye.

"Ross, over this way!"

I ran, Ross following.

We found Ken huddled under a small rock overhang wrapped in his shiny space blanket. He looked gaunt, his clothes smelled of smoke and rotten fish, but he was alive. And he had a smile on his face.

"Ken!" I hugged him tight. "I'm so happy we finally found you."

When I let him go, I tore off his tattered space blanket. "Let's get you to the plane."

"You won't get an argument from me," Ken said feebly. "I'll need some help. I think I broke my ankle."

We lifted Ken to his feet with Ross serving as a human crutch on one side and with Ken's arm wrapped around my shoulder to stabilize the other side. Somehow, we managed to hobble, three abreast, down the bank to the plane and to boost him through the door onto the seat.

Once inside, although weak, Ken managed to nibble on Pilot Bread from our emergency food supply and to sip most of a bottle of water before falling asleep. Despite the warmth of the cabin and the constraint of his seatbelt, he'd managed to curl up into a semi-fetal position on his seat. Ross tucked a blanket snugly around him, and I'd turned up the heat for the trip back.

Ross turned to me and smiled. "I'm so glad we found him."

"Me too, Ross, me too!" Tears blurred my vision as we headed for home.

Chapter Forty

Detective Diaz and the paramedics met us at Merrill Field. I'd called them and Paige Abbott during our return flight. Paige, ecstatic at the news Ken was alive, promised to be on the first plane she could catch out of Kotzebue.

While the paramedics loaded Ken in the ambulance, Detective Diaz took me aside. "I see the evidence we shared with you yielded the desired result. Congratulations."

"Yes. We owe you a big one. Hanratty's map led us right to Ken."

"You helped me out, too. I was loudly criticized for cooperating with you. Some of my peers claimed you should be considered a suspect and the last person to share anything with during an investigation. Even though I saw the same evidence you did, it didn't mean anything to me. I'd planned to investigate the map further, but I had no idea of the urgency."

I smiled. "I can understand. I didn't know what I was looking for until I saw it, and you had a smaller piece of the total picture than I did."

"He's in rough shape. Did he tell you anything useful about what happened?"

"Some. Ken said Hanratty landed his plane nearby while he was setting up camp. Ace walked over to him, seemed friendly and then surprised him by picking up a shovel and clobbering him. It knocked him out cold. When he came to, both their planes were gone."

"So Hanratty had help?"

"Apparently, although Ken said he didn't see anyone fly in with him. Said he figured he'd been unconscious for a couple of hours and woke up alone and hog-tied. It took him a full day to work himself free."

"Impressive that he managed to survive almost a month out there alone."

"It is. He'd spent a lot of time prospecting in the wilderness, and it didn't hurt that salmon were running and blueberries were ripe. Ken's tough and smart, he proved that, but it has taken a toll. My guess is you won't be able to talk to him until tomorrow. His ankle may require surgery. The doctors will also want to assess his head injury and dehydration."

"I'll check with the hospital staff and have them call me when he's stable." He glanced up at Ross. "You have anything to add?"

"Not really, except Ken felt well enough to ask me to bring him some clean clothes."

Diaz laughed. "Sounds like he can still think straight. Maybe I'll see you again at the hospital."

We tied down the plane and threw out our trash. I picked up my emergency blanket that had covered Ken and tossed it in the car.

"Whew. Definitely smells ripe. I think I could use a shower, too," I said.

"I agree, but let's run by Walmart first so I can pick up some underwear and sweats to leave for Ken at the hospital."

"Good idea. I'm sure he'll want to be presentable when his mom gets here in the morning. Those hospital gowns won't cut it."

"The press will probably show up. Don't think he'd want to be so exposed."

"You're right about that. He's a humble guy. I just remembered. I need to call Shawna! She'll be so thrilled to see him."

At home, with the blanket and our clothes in the washer, Ross and I jumped in the shower together. "You know, your dad will be discharged soon. We won't be able to act this way much longer," Ross said.

I smiled as I washed his torso. "We'll figure something out."

Later, after we dressed, I fed Tiger while Ross made omelets. We carried them into the family room and settled in front of the television. After eating, I picked up the phone. "I'd better make a couple of phone calls before Ken's story hits the news." I dialed Dad's cell first.

"Dad, I've got great news! Ross and I found my missing student today. He's half starved, but he's alive and he'll recover."

"That's wonderful, cupcake. I knew you could do it. Jack will be very happy."

"Thanks, that reminds me of something I need to do. I've got to go, but I wanted you to be the first to know. Hope to see you tomorrow, Dad."

"Before you go, I have news too. They've moved me to rehab and say I can probably go home as soon as I get my balance back. Can't be soon enough for me."

"Or me. Glad you're making such good progress. I'll talk to you more tomorrow."

Ross reached for my hand as I hung up.

I smiled at him as I let go and reached for the phone again. "I still need to call Norm at the FBI. He may have already heard the news from Diaz, but I also want to ask him something."

I dialed, expecting to get his answering machine, but instead he picked up.

"Beri. I hear you found your pilot. Is Ken okay?"

I couldn't help but smile into the phone. "Yes. The word must be out. I'd hoped his mother would get here first."

"How is he?"

"He'll be fine once he's had time to recuperate." I paused. "I have a question for you. Did you or the troopers involved in investigating the chop shop examine the plane Ken was flying?"

"Enough to see it will never fly again."

"Tell me about it. That's what my insurance adjuster's assessment was, too. My rates are going to be out of sight next year."

"You have my sympathy."

"Did you find a tracker attached to the plane?"

"No, but we weren't looking for one, either. Why?"

"That's how we located Ken. We found a GPS print out at the Hanratty crime scene."

"Hmm... I'll have the guys hunt for one. I know they found the emergency locator beacon inside the shop. It was in working order, but had been switched off."

"It seems there's still a few missing pieces to the puzzle," I said.

Chapter Forty-one

Ross left to catch up on work at his office. I tried to relax, but felt too restless. I wanted to talk to Jack, but had no way to reach him without making an expensive international call to his father's phone. Deciding exercise would help settle me, I grabbed my gym bag and drove to the Alaska Club. I hadn't done much cardio lately.

The club appeared quieter than usual, which was fine with me. I didn't feel like conversation anyway. I picked up a towel at the desk and headed straight for the locker room. I'd almost made it when someone called my name.

"Beri. I didn't expect to see you here," Norm said. "When we spoke earlier, I pictured you at home taking it easy."

"I was, but I couldn't calm my nerves and decided a work-out might help."

"Usually does." He held up a racquet. "Any chance I could interest you in a game of racquetball? I have a court reserved, but my partner cancelled at the last minute."

"Um, I'm rusty, but I think I have my racquet and goggles in the car. I'll meet you in five minutes."

"Court two. Prepare for battle."

After three games, we called it quits. Norm proved himself the better player. I managed to win one game and that was a nail biter.

"Nasty serve," Norm said. "Where did you learn that?"

I laughed. "I had to learn it for self-preservation growing up playing against my father. I figured out early on that if he couldn't return my serve, I could catch my breath."

We lowered ourselves down to sit on the court floor, leaned against the back wall, legs stretched out straight in front of us.

Norm turned to me. "Did Diaz tell you they've taken the owner of the SUV you spotted into custody? Word is that he's talking."

"No! When did this happen? I spoke to him this afternoon."

"He called just before I left the office."

"Do you know if they've learned anything from him?"

"No, you'll have to ask Diaz about that." He bounced a ball lightly in the air with his racquet. "On another note, we learned that your friend, Kaitlin's stolen plane's VIN number had been replaced with a data plate from a similar wrecked plane. It appears your attackers planned to sell it."

"So they weren't going to part it out, but how could they get away with selling it?"

"While it's true a complete plane is worth less than the sum of its parts, in this case they apparently decided not to bother taking it apart. I'd guess because the plane was so new, and possibly, because they were afraid they were running out of time. They probably realized I'd entered it into our stolen plane data base."

"I'm sure Kaitlin's happy they left it intact. It was stolen almost immediately after it was delivered to her." I paused. "What I don't understand is how they could get away with switching data plates."

"When a plane is totaled, it's supposed to be reported to the FAA as out of commission. Unfortunately, this too often doesn't happen, and crooks can retrieve it or even buy it and use the data plate and retrievable parts with no one the wiser."

"Good to know. It reminds me I need to formally report a couple of totaled planes myself, although the FAA already knows about one of them."

"You do that. We also found an abundant supply of counterfeit boxes they were planning to use to market parts to unsuspecting buyers. We think they were even relabeling car parts for use in Super Cubs. Some parts are similar to those used in automobiles, but FAA approved parts are the only type legal to use in aviation." Norm sighed. "This bunch didn't miss a beat. We found boxes of smuggled, unapproved foreign parts ready for relabeling as well."

"Wow." I pushed myself up off the floor. "I think we've stayed past our scheduled court time. Thanks for the games and the information. I had no idea a parts scam could be so sophisticated. They must have been making a fortune."

"I think they were. Unapproved parts are a big problem in general aviation and an even bigger problem in commercial and military aviation. It doesn't get much press because no one wants to think their airline may have installed counterfeit avionics from China or a de-icing system from a cannibalized decommissioned airliner."

"But the FAA does approve recycling some parts."

"Yes, of course, but the regulations for doing so are strict, and a clear paper trail must be provided to the buyer. What I'm talking about are parts that can be removed and sold by a scammer with an electric screwdriver."

"Are you close to making any arrests in the case?"

"Getting closer every day."

Chapter Forty-two

Dad sat in a chair eating oatmeal when I tracked him down in his new rehab quarters.

"No wonder you're anxious to go home. The cuisine isn't up to your standards."

"It's not that bad. At least they don't use instant oatmeal."

"I hope not. So how are they going about rehabilitating you?"

Dad laughed. "I offer them lots of opportunities, cupcake, but they're mostly having me work on my walking and balance. I'm still unsteady on my feet and the last thing I need is to take a bad fall."

"Agreed. Should we move your bed downstairs for a while?"

"No! I can manage the stairs if I hold onto the rail. I'll be good as new in a few weeks anyway."

"I like the sound of that." I gave him a hug. "Gotta get to work. I'll stop back as soon as I can."

Instead of going directly to the office, I stopped in at the ICU, hoping to see Ken. It turned out he'd been moved out to a room a floor down, and I found him holding court in a room full of visitors. I walked into the crowd and squeezed his hand, taking care to avoid the one with the IV attached.

"Glad to see you seem to be doing better today."

"Thanks to you, Beri, I'm feeling wicked good."

"Not good enough for this many visitors," a nurse standing in the doorway said. "Do you think we could break this up into shifts? Maximum of three at a time and keep it short."

Most of the herd said farewell, leaving just Paige, Shawna and me standing around the bed. Ken sported a cast on his foot that went half way up his calf. He'd cleaned up and shaved his beard, and looked more like his old self—only thinner.

Shawna moved to my side of Ken's bed and gave me a hug. "Thank you so much. It's a miracle you finally found him."

"The credit goes to Ken for managing to stay alive all this time," I said. "Jack told me he had skills and knew he'd survive, but I have to admit I worried he wouldn't be able to hang on long enough for us to find him."

I moved the only chair in the room over so Paige could sit as I turned to face Ken. "These two really helped me search for you. We tried everything we could think of. Your mom and I flew a lot of miles together taking pictures of the terrain, and Shawna pushed us to ignore the phony flight plan and figure out where you really went."

Ken smiled. "I must admit I'd about decided I was a goner when I slipped in the stream and broke my ankle. Before that, I'd managed to live off the land with help from my survival vest and pocket knife."

"When do you think you can go home?" I asked.

Paige jumped in. "The doctor said I could take him home to Boston in another day or two," Paige said.

Ken reached over and placed his hand on his mother's arm. "I appreciate that, Mom, but Shawna's agreed to move into my apartment with me temporarily until I get my strength back."

"What about Nico? Won't it get a little crowded?" Paige asked.

"He'll be gone for another month. By then, I should be in good shape."

"Speaking of Nico," I said. "What's the story about your nugget? We understand he was trying to sell it."

Ken laughed. "Nico? No, he offered to get it appraised as a favor to me. I needed to insure it before I lent it to the museum."

"Museum?" Paige asked. "What museum?"

"The Anchorage Museum. They planned an exhibit on gold prospecting in Alaska and asked if they could include it."

"Another mystery solved," Paige said. "We tried unsuccessfully to reach Nico to ask him about it. What do you plan to do with your nugget when you get it back?"

"Since it would be too flashy to wear as a belt buckle," Ken said with a smirk, "I'll probably sell it. If my application works out, I'll need all the money I can get to maintain my gold claim."

Paige frowned. "So now you want to be a gold miner?"

"Don't worry, Mom. I plan to finish school, too."

I said my good-byes and left the hospital, happy to see this family together. I glanced at my watch when I reached the car. Still early enough I could call Jack. The time difference between Alaska and Germany added to the complication of calling.

The call went through without a hitch. Dennis seemed surprised to hear my voice, but told me they were currently in Friedrichshafen and planned to stay a couple of days. He turned the phone over to Jack.

"Mom, I'm having so much fun. Yesterday, I spotted a diving bird with a red head at the lake. I'd never seen one like it. I took a picture so I could look it up when I got home. Later, a lady in the restaurant said it was a pochard. She told me they see a lot of them this time of year."

"Sounds exciting."

"And Dad and I are going to ride on a zeppelin tomorrow. It's kinda like a blimp. Wish you could go, too. The girls are too scared to go. They're going shopping instead."

"Jack, I can't talk long, but I wanted to tell you the good news. We found Ken! He's alive and he's going to be okay."

"Really? That's great! Thank you for telling me. I can't wait to see him."

I told him briefly about what had happened to his grandpa, but that he was going to be okay, too.

"I'll tell you all about it when you get back. I'd better sign off for now. It was wonderful to hear your voice. I love you and miss you a lot."

"I love you too, Mom."

I disconnected and drove to the office with a smile on my face.

Chapter Forty-three

Sully called me on my cell phone as I loaded the twin, preparing to fly a long-standing job in the Aleutians. The weather looked promising, although iffy, which was the usual state of affairs in that area of the state. The job had been pending most of the summer as I'd awaited the rare day the skies cleared over the project. This could be it, so I didn't welcome a change in plans.

"Beri, I have news," Sully said. "I've been in conversation with my contact at the NTSB. He needs to interview you and your mechanic as soon as possible."

"You caught me just as I was preparing to leave for Cold Bay. Can we arrange it as soon as I return?"

"I don't think so. You need to drop everything and set this up *now*. We can't let time drag on this. I'm afraid a crisis of some sort will intervene and distract their attention. We need to do this today."

I sighed. If only the good weather could be as easily rescheduled. "Okay. Tell me when and where, and Dean and I will be there."

"My office. One hour."

"Yes sir."

Sully's contact turned out to be the Chief NTSB Inspector for the state of Alaska, Morris Benson.

"Glad to meet both of you," he said and shook our hands. "Dean, I understand you have a theory about the cause of Beri's crash landing."

"I do," Dean said. "Upon examining the fuel lines, I found remnants of a plastic zip-lock bag."

"Did anyone witness your finding it?"

"Yes sir. I made this discovery at the helicopter hangar where I'd had the wreckage taken. Several of the mechanics working there observed me finding it."

"So your theory of the crash is…?" Morris asked.

"I think the baggie held water. The plastic slowly dissolved in the fuel tank, contaminating the fuel with water and causing the engine to quit. It's also possible fragments of plastic clogged the fuel lines, although I couldn't confirm that."

"How long do you estimate it would take for the plastic to dissolve?"

Dean glanced at Morris, then away, a mannerism of respect consistent with his Yup'ik heritage. "I experimented submerging water filled baggies in aviation fuel and timing the process. Results varied, but I'd estimate several hours."

"So if your theory is correct, the bag could have been dropped in the tank the night before?"

"It must have been, because the plane wasn't left unattended the morning of the crash."

Morris wrote something down in a notepad, then asked, "How would the culprit have known the pilot wouldn't have discovered the water during her preflight check?"

Dean shrugged. "I don't know. He must have taken a chance on the timing."

"Quite a theory you have there. I'd like to see the evidence you found."

Dean shot me a sideways glance. "I turned it over to the FAA inspector. He didn't appear to place much importance on it so I took some photographs." He took an envelope from his jacket and held it out.

Benson reached for the pictures and tucked them into his shirt pocket. "I hadn't heard about any of this until Sully called me, but I'll certainly look into it." He turned to me. "Do you have anything to add, Ms. Quinn?"

"No, Dean covered it well," I said. "But a thought did just occur to me. I recently noticed laundry bluing and a rack of test tubes at the work site of a person who may have been involved. I thought it odd at the time, but now I wonder if the water placed in the baggie might have been tinted the same blue color as the fuel. It would have made it harder to catch if there was any pre-flight leakage."

"That's a new one to me. Has anyone interviewed this person about that possibility?" Morris asked.

"No, I'm afraid that's impossible. He's dead. Murdered."

"Who was he?"

"Ace Hanratty," I said, "the owner of the business we suspected of selling mislabeled aviation parts."

By the time I returned to the office and checked the weather, the ceiling over my project had dropped below minimums. Not only couldn't I take pictures, I couldn't safely fly to the project. I wondered if I'd ever finish this job. Weather on the Aleutian Chain was notoriously bad. Rumor is that school is cancelled in Cold Bay on the rare days the sun shines. The opposite of a snow day.

I unloaded the plane and started thinking about lunch when my cell phone rang again.

"Sully here. I need you."

"What's happening now?"

Moe's been busy. He contacted the police and they agreed to accompany an FAA inspector to inventory Hanratty's stock and check for counterfeit parts. They suggested it would be helpful for you and Dean to accompany them."

"Are you sure Larry Lindsey, the local FAA inspector, will agree to that? We're not on the best of terms."

"It's not Lindsey I'm talking about. Moe asked someone from the Washington DC office to review the case. He'll be there. We'll meet you at Hanratty's place at two o'clock. Bring Dean."

Chapter Forty-four

It was a short drive for Dean and me, so it was not surprising we were the first to arrive. At least I thought we were first before I spotted a black Land Rover parked behind the building and partially hidden by a dumpster. I drove over to take a look and noticed the crime scene tape fluttering from the edge of the open back door.

"They must already be here," I said.

"I don't know, I think that's Lindsey's vehicle. I noticed it the day he visited our hangar. Maybe we should wait for the police," Dean said.

At that moment, Lindsey appeared in the doorway carrying two boxes in his arms. He spotted us, dropped the cartons and pulled out a gun.

I shifted to reverse, gunned the accelerator and flew backwards across the parking lot. "Get down!" I yelled to Dean.

I shifted to drive and raced forward toward the front of the building. As I rounded the corner, a police sedan followed by two other cars drove in.

I leaned on my horn, attempting to alert them to danger as the Land Rover roared behind me. A shot rang out and my side mirror shattered.

A Ford sedan slammed to a sideways stop, blocking the exit to the parking lot. Diaz and another officer jumped out of their vehicle and returned fire.

Lindsey ducked out of sight. He flashed his headlights and yelled, "Don't shoot. I'm dropping my gun out the window."

Diaz shouted, "Show us your hands. Put both out the window where I can see them."

Lindsey complied.

Diaz jerked the door to the Land Rover open while the other officer covered him with his gun drawn. Diaz kicked Lindsey's gun away from the vehicle and yanked him out, frisked him and handcuffed his hands behind him.

After locking him into the back of his Ford, Diaz walked over to talk to me. "One more crime scene to process," he said and sighed. "Guess we'll have to reschedule the inventory inspection."

"I think we arrived just in time to prevent Lindsey from removing the evidence. Check the rear door. It was open when we got here and he dropped several boxes he was taking. I think he packed things up for us."

Diaz nodded. "I will, thanks. You're becoming a regular at these. Might have to sign up for criminal justice classes soon."

I laughed and rotated my shoulders backward to relax the tension. "Never. Planes are my passion. You can keep the criminals."

Returning to the office, I noticed my hands jiggling on the steering wheel. Earlier, I'd suspected my tires were out of balance when they didn't track straight. Now I was sure of it. I dropped Dean off and drove to my tire center. Before handing over the keys to my Subaru, I picked up the stack of mail I'd left on the passenger seat.

Once inside, I found an empty plastic chair and sat down to wait. I sorted through the mail until I found the latest edition of the *Journal of the American Society of Photogrammetry and Remote Sensing*. Deciding to use my wait time productively, I flipped to the table of contents to see if any of the articles interested me and quickly struck pay dirt. The third title down, "Clash of the Titans, a Battle for Mapping Supremacy," caught my eye. I turned to the correct page and found myself captivated, reading the article from start to finish without stopping.

The author detailed the power struggle between Alex Veronin, President of Cartos, and Steele Zevan, CEO of Combined Data Collections. Both corporations were trying to capture the market west of the Mississippi by buying out individual companies in the selected states.

Alex's behavior began to make sense. Alaska offered a potentially large market. He'd hate for his competition to control it. While other Alaskan mapping companies existed, Anchorage was a business center for the state, and Quinn Aviation and Aerial Images didn't have many competitors of consequence in Anchorage. I picked up the phone, found the corporate phone number and placed a call to Mr. Zevan.

Chapter Forty-five

About two hours later, Detective Diaz called me. "Good, I'm glad you're in," he said. "Can I get you to come down to the precinct? I'd like to have you take a look at a line-up for me."

"Sure," I said. "What kind of line-up?"

"Just want to know if any of the faces are familiar to you."

"No problem. When is it scheduled?"

"Now, if you can get here in the next fifteen minutes."

"I'll be there."

It took only ten minutes to make the drive. When I approached Diaz's desk, Norm was sitting next to him drinking coffee.

"Hello. I didn't expect to see you here."

"This is an unusual case. It involves us, the police and even the troopers since you were kidnapped and your plane was recovered in their jurisdiction," Norm said.

"Shall we get started?" Diaz asked. "Right this way."

Diaz led us into a viewing room. "I'll call each individual to step forward and repeat a sentence we've provided them. If you see the person you say kidnapped you, please identify him." He picked up a microphone and spoke into it. "Please send them in."

Five men filed into the room behind one-way glass.

I knew the moment I saw him that number two was the man who'd accosted me at the chop shop, but I waited for the process to play out.

"Number one step forward. Please read the sentence you've been given."

The first man did as asked. Diaz looked at me, and I shook my head.

"Number two. You know what to do," Diaz said into the microphone.

Number two stepped forward and remained silent.

"Repeat the sentence on the card you were given."

The man sighed and read in a quiet monotone, "Be careful of this bitch, she's dangerous."

"That's him. He's trying to disguise his voice, but I'd know him anywhere. I don't see the other man up there, though."

"Thanks. You've been a big help," Norm said. After he reached over and shook my hand, he did the same with Diaz. "Appreciate the teamwork here."

"Have you found the other guy?" I asked.

"We don't have him in custody at this time. We're both working on it," Diaz said.

"I assume you can tell me who the owner of the SUV is now," I said. "Was it this man?"

"No," Diaz said. "It belongs to Marianne Hermann, Lindsey's girlfriend."

"The woman who presided over my FAA hearing? She was driving it?" I felt like I had been punched in the gut.

"We hope to sort that out after we get this fellow to cooperate."

"I have some answers for you," Norm said later that afternoon when he stopped by my office. "Unfortunately, I also have more questions."

"Have a seat. Let's hear what you have."

"Your captor asked for an attorney and clammed up completely until he found out we had Lindsey in custody as well. Diaz also tracked down the other fellow from the chop shop."

"The skinny guy with glasses?"

"Yep. Turns out he's Lindsey's younger brother. When we pitted them all against each other, the story came spilling out."

"That's great. What did they say?"

"Lindsey was the mastermind of the parts scheme, as we suspected. When you showed up at the chop shop, they called Lindsey and he ordered his brother flown out immediately. Didn't want him implicated in the scheme."

"So that's why they left me alone. He was trying to protect his brother."

"I guess. Seems the brother kept the books and distribution records, but otherwise didn't get his hands dirty. At least that's what Lindsey says."

"How about who drove the SUV and shot Buzz?"

"That was Lindsey himself. He says he was alone in the vehicle and wanted to scare Dean off. He felt the report you filed would fall apart without Dean's testimony. He drove his girlfriend's spare vehicle because he thought you'd seen his Range Rover when he'd visited your hangar. He drove it the day he killed Hanratty for the same reason. Apparently, it wasn't used much and was usually parked in her garage."

"Okay, so that explains the SUV sitting there, but I don't understand why he wanted to kill Hanratty in the first place. Was he blackmailing him?"

"According to Lindsey, Hanratty was becoming unstable and too hard to control. His attack on your dad was the final straw. Lindsey figured if he didn't take drastic measures, Hanratty would eventually bring the whole enterprise down."

I shook my head. "Senseless. So, what happens now?"

"Lindsey is being held on murder charges, and his two accomplices on kidnapping and racketeering charges."

"It's over then. Veronin wasn't involved?"

"Diaz's men tracked down the thug you shot in your office by checking emergency room records. Hospitals are required to report gunshot wounds. The guy says Veronin ordered him to keep pressuring you to sell your business. He only planned to scare you."

"He did a good job of that."

"He's been charged with assault, but has already been bailed out. Not sure if the charge will stick, since he was the injured party." Norm smiled.

"So, this whole nightmare turns out to be a convergence of forces centered simultaneously on my business and family?"

"Seems that way. Lucky you were up to the challenge."

I laughed. *Little did he know.*

Chapter Forty-six

The next morning, Alex Veronin strolled into my office. Angie and I jerked to attention.

"Relax, ladies. I'm here on a goodwill mission." He motioned to the classroom door. "Beri, could I speak to you privately for a moment?"

I stood and walked to the classroom. "I'll won't be long, Angie."

Once inside, Veronin closed the door. "I know this is awkward for you. It is for me also, but I wanted to personally apologize to you. When I didn't hear back from you and had to leave, I asked my employees to continue encouraging you to sell. I didn't, however, mean for them to use gestapo tactics."

"They stormed my office and threatened me, they stalked my family and tasered my dog. It was far from friendly persuasion," I said.

He sat on the corner of one of the tables. "They exasperate me. I don't know what they were thinking. I bailed them out, but they are no longer in my employ."

Veronin pulled a small box from his jacket pocket. "I hope you'll accept this token of my regret for what we put you through."

"No. I don't want it. You don't need to do that."

"I feel I do. If you open the box, you'll find a pair of tourmaline earrings I chose because they would complement the lovely green dress you wore to the gala. Emeralds would have been better, but I doubted you would accept a gift that expensive."

"Very thoughtful of you, but you no longer have a reason to butter me up. I've recently agreed to sell my company to your competitor."

"Yes, I heard. I deserved that. My apology now is simply an apology. I don't expect anything from you in return." He closed the lid and placed the box on the table. "Nice knowing you, Beri," he said and left.

I sat down for the first time since entering the room. Veronin was a strange man. A contradiction. He was attractive, but he also repelled. His apology sounded sincere, but was it? Still, I couldn't resist picking up the box and peeking inside. The drop-style earrings were gorgeous, their green hue a match to my dress, as he'd said. Stranger things had surely happened to me, but I couldn't remember when.

I left the classroom to find Angie staring at me expectantly.

"Well?" she said.

"He apologized. He made nice."

"You're buying that?"

"Yes. He has nothing to gain."

"If you say so." Angie stood up from her desk. "I think I'll take an early lunch."

I took the box from my pocket and held it out to her. "Here. I have something for you."

Angie gave me a quizzical glance as she took the box and opened it. "Wow. What did I do to deserve this?"

"You've hung in there with me. I appreciate your support through our tough times together. Just one caveat—please, don't wear them to work."

"Did he give them to you?" Angie lifted one of the earrings and held it up to the light. "Never mind. I don't want to know. Thank you."

Chapter Forty-seven

I stood on the boardwalk of Potter's Marsh, staring out toward the mountains. The birds weren't particularly active today. A lone tundra swan paddled in a wide circle on the water, searching for dinner.

Ross joined me and put his arm around my shoulder. "Good meeting place. Glad you suggested it."

"One of my favorite spots to relax and think life's big thoughts."

"What deep thoughts are you thinking about today?"

"Some especially important ones. I finally realized if I refused to give up my business I could lose everything truly important to me. Dad thought I was crazy not to accept Veronin's offer, but I couldn't do that after everything that had happened. I decided to sell, but not to Veronin. His competitor's offer was lower, but fair. Now that it's done, I'm planning to travel to Arizona once Dad is on his feet. I'll spend the winter there to be near Jack." I turned to face Ross. "It's a bittersweet decision in a lot of ways."

"Congratulations on the sale. It sounds like you've thought it through. Wish I could be happier about it, but I'm going to miss you too much."

"I know. That's the hard part. Leaving you and leaving Alaska, but I plan to be back and I'll bring Jack with me as soon as school is out."

"I'll be here. Anxious for your return."

"Jack needs me whether he knows it or not."

"I understand, Beri." He tilted my chin up and gave me a lingering kiss.

"Are you open to a business proposal?" I asked.

"Business?"

"Yes. I'd like to invest in your company. Join you as a partner. With two of us, we could expand operations next summer."

"I'd like that."

"Do you think we could include Dean and Angie in the deal? Assuming they'd agree to it, of course."

"Dean would be great. Angie might give me some heartburn, but I could handle it."

I laughed. "Angie will keep you on your financial toes, but you'll be lucky to have her."

"With you as a partner, I can learn to put up with anything."

I gave Ross a squeeze. "I like the sound of that."

"What finally convinced you to sell?"

"Jack. I can't leave him like my mother left me. True, it's his choice to be with his dad at this point, but I need to be close in case something goes wrong or he changes his mind. Selling gave me the freedom to manage that."

"He's a great kid. I hope he realizes how lucky he is to have you." Ross took my hand in both of his. "It's a deal. We'll let the lawyers work out the details, but let's shake on it, partner."

"Sounds good. Now let's go tell Dad."

Ross groaned.

I gently punched his shoulder and ended up in his arms again. For the moment, life was good. My world had changed, but finally prospects for the future were bright.

Readers, watch for another mystery coming from Toni Niesen in 2018…

If you enjoyed *Parts Unknown*, you may enjoy these other mysteries from Written Dreams Publishing!

Death Nosh

Book 3 of the Noshes Up North Culinary Mystery Series

Mary Grace Murphy

Someone is sneaking into houses, committing murders, and escaping without a trace. Can Nell Bailey convince the police to take her seriously?

The police chief thinks it's the normal passing of senior citizens when people start to turn up dead in a small Wisconsin town. But Nell Bailey, food blogger and restaurant reviewer, has a different opinion.

To further complicate her life, Sam, her gentleman friend, isn't acting very gentlemanly. Plus, his plans don't include Nell investigating any more murders. Can she hold her own against two men, Sam Ryan and Chief Vance, who are so accustomed to doing things their way?

Freewheel

Book 2 of the Tri-Angles Series

Katharine M. Nohr

Freewheel takes readers for a spin in Hawaii in the real world of personal injury litigation, where the drama takes place outside the courtroom.

Olympic gold medalist, Ryan Peterson can't seem to get a break. He was ousted from professional cycling for doping. After he switched sports to triathlon, he was blasted by the tabloid press for allegedly causing an accident that wiped out his competitors. In an effort to redeem himself, Ryan starts the Freewheel Movement to help homeless and isolated people financially and emotionally. Although Freewheel is an instant success and Ryan becomes a television talk show regular, his bad luck continues. He's sued for allegedly causing the death of a competitor in a Hawaii triathlon, and no matter what he does, he can't convince the beautiful claims adjuster, Alexia Moore, to go out with him.

Young and ambitious new attorney Zana West is hired to represent Ryan and provide him a defense in the lawsuit, but by doing so, her relationship with Jerry Hirano, T.V. star of "Fighting in Paradise," is threatened. Will Zana be able to help Ryan get his life back, and keep her relationship together?

Death By G-String

Book 1 of the Coyote Canyon Ukulele Club Mystery Series

C.C. Harrison

Can Viva Winter find the truth before it's too late?

The Coyote Canyon Ladies Ukulele Club is gearing up for a ukulele competition when their flamboyant star player, Kiki Jacquenette, is found strangled to death with a G-string. Not only is a first place win in jeopardy, the entire folk music festival is put on the verge of collapse. A murderer on the loose is sure to keep tourists away.

Chronicle editor Viva Winter had hoped to make Coyote Canyon the folk music capitol of the Colorado mountains, and was also trying to raise money to help repay the townspeople bilked by her father's phony investment scheme. With much to gain by Kiki's death, Viva soon comes under suspicion, so she must uncover the truth before her whole life turns into one sour note, and a tourist trade boom falls flat.

Acknowledgements

Many thanks to the many people who helped in the research of this book. Their expertise is considerable, mine less so. All errors are mine alone.
Aviation: Warren Niesen, pilot and husband extraordinaire, Roger Carter, Bob Nobmann and Bob Seiler, great pilots all.

Flight Instruction: Jamie Patterson Simes of Sky Trek Alaska

Photography: Warren Penny and Warren Niesen

Beta Readers: Gwen Robinson, Susan Budavari, Monty Fox and Kathy Anderson. Your feedback and suggestions were invaluable.

Fellow Members of Alaska and Desert Sleuths Sisters in Crime: Your support and camaraderie kept me going. Special thanks to C.C. Harrison for her insightful critiques.

About the Author

Toni Niesen lived in Alaska for twenty-four years. She worked in public health in Anchorage, and lived the life of a pilot vicariously through the exploits of her husband and friends. She is the author of short stories, three of which were published in Desert Sleuth anthologies. *Parts Unknown* is her debut novel. She currently lives in Scottsdale, Arizona with her husband, grandson, and Boston Terrier, Sushi. To learn more about Toni Niesen and her books, visit writtendreams.com, or find her on social media.